The Beach at Herculaneum
A Novel

SUSAN G. MUTH

iUniverse, Inc.
Bloomington

The Beach at Herculaneum
A Novel

iUniverse books may be ordered through booksellers or by contacting:

iUniverse
1663 Liberty Drive
Bloomington, IN 47403
www.iuniverse.com
1-800-Authors (1-800-288-4677)

Library of Congress Control Number: 2012920380

ISBN: 978-1-4759-5912-3 (sc)
ISBN: 978-1-4759-5911-6 (hc)
ISBN: 978-1-4759-5910-9 (e)

Printed in the United States of America

iUniverse rev. date: 11/27/2012

For Vic and Loree, who gave me the courage
and for Vasili, who gave me the encouragement

Acknowledgments

My heartfelt thanks to my sister, Victoria Dahmes, for the time and energy she spent helping me hone my manuscript. When she'd suggest a change, I'd recoil, think about it for a day or two, then find a way to make the change while keeping the concept intact. Through this process, *Herculaneum* became reader-friendly. It was great.

Thanks also to Mignon Fahr, one of the great unpublished authors of our time, and to all my fellow writers at the Mandeville Public Library who helped midwife this novel into the world. Without all of you, this manuscript might have dried to dust in my file drawer and never been read by anyone.

Finally, I want to thank Sarah Disbrow, Rebekka Potter, and all the people at iUniverse for their painstaking attention to my novel and their encouragement to keep refining it into its best form. After years of frustration, it was wonderful just to get someone to actually read my work; getting specific feedback and person-to-person discussion restored my confidence and made me want to start my next book.

Palla

Stola

Intima
(Shift)

HERCULANEUM MAP

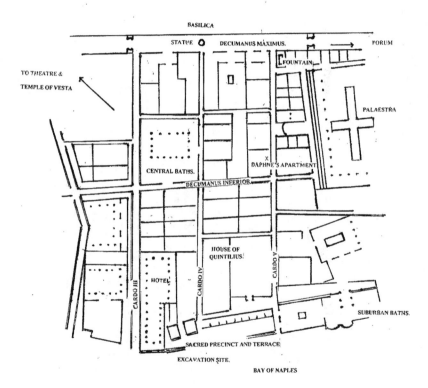

BASILICA

STATUE ○   DECUMANUS MAXIMUS.   FORUM

TO THEATRE &
TEMPLE OF VESTA

FOUNTAIN

PALAESTRA

CENTRAL BATHS.

X
DAPHNE'S APARTMENT

DECUMANUS INFERIOR.

HOUSE OF
QUINTILIUS.

CARDO III   HOTEL   CARDO IV   CARDO V

SUBURBAN BATHS.

SACRED PRECINCT AND TERRACE

EXCAVATION SITE.

BAY OF NAPLES

Author's Note to the Reader

I 've tried my best to present the life and death of first century Herculaneum accurately, but at times I found myself weighing historical authenticity against dramatic effect. For example, the actual eruption of Vesuvius started around one o'clock in the afternoon and lasted until just after midnight. Pompeii was downwind and suffocated under the rain of ash and pumice within a few hours. Herculaneum's end was more violent. When the eruption column finally collapsed that night, the glowing avalanche that followed swept over the town, destroying it in one swoop.

However, putting you through eleven hours of excruciating detail, in the minute-to-minute focus I've chosen for this story, seemed not only tedious but detrimental to pace and flow. So I compressed the time frame, starting at midday and culminating at an unspecified time after nightfall. Trust me, it improves the read.

I also chose to compromise on some of the Latin. For instance, the common greeting "Sal-we" would have been spelled "salve," but I could envision you saying to yourself, "Salve? Like an ointment?" Likewise, the vocative form of "Marcus" would have been "Marce," but I feared you might read it "Marcie" or "Marse," so I spelled it "Mar-ce" to look more like the actual pronunciation—"Mar-kay." Classical Latin had no silent vowels and no soft consonants, nor did they use contractions the way we do. They sometimes shortened longer words, but they didn't use apostrophes in place of letters or syllables. They would not, for example, have said things like "they didn't."

As for the various garments and locations mentioned in the ancient segments, rather than take time in the midst of my narrative to explain each term, I thought I'd better just draw you a couple of pictures. You're welcome.

Chapter 2

Father Martin had heard my sins and given me Holy Communion since I was a child. He'd been there when I was sixteen, the day I'd come back from shopping with my friends to find a squad car in the driveway. *We're very sorry, Miss Ryan, but there's been an accident ... sailboat registered to your father ... lightning struck the mast ... your parents, your brother Tommy ... calling off the search ... is there someone we can call?*

Father Martin was the only living person in the world I still trusted. Yet, today his familiar profile, seen through the confessional's carved grillwork, seemed vague and somehow alien in the dim light. My insides quivered, and I felt sick as I leaned back against the confessional's inner wall. I drew in a ragged breath and began.

"Forgive me, Father, for I have sinned. It's been four weeks since my last confession."

"How are you, Anne?" came the soft, slightly raspy voice.

"I don't know, Father. I can't ..." The words caught in my throat, and I stopped, took a couple of deep breaths.

"All right, take a moment. There's no hurry."

"I have sinned," I tried again, "but I don't understand."

"What kind of sin do you think you've committed?"

"I don't know," I said wearily. "I don't know, Father, but it must have been something terrible, because God has turned his back on me."

"God never turns his back on us, Anne. But sometimes we turn our backs on him. Do you think you may have done that?"

"I've done everything, Father. I've prayed, I've gone to Mass, I've said Hail Marys until my tongue is numb, but …" I took in a long breath. "But I can't reach him. He's just not there."

"He's there, Anne."

"Well," I almost snapped, "I can't find him."

"You sound angry," Father Martin said evenly.

I sighed and hesitated.

"Anne," he prompted, "is there something else?"

"I had a dream, Father. An awful dream. I went to the Blessed Mother for help, but …"

I could hear Father Martin's soft breathing through the grill as he waited.

I gathered myself and plunged on. "She was made of stone. She spoke to me in Latin. She said I didn't belong there. I was afraid of her, and I ran."

He was quiet for a moment, and then he said, "You had bad dreams after your family died, too, didn't you?"

With that quick slash the old wound gaped open. I hated him for saying it. "That was different," I hissed through the grate. "I blamed myself."

"Yes, I remember."

Suddenly I was a grieving teenage girl again. "I should have been with them. I wanted to go to the mall. I couldn't be bothered to go sailing with my family that day."

"And so you survived."

"Yes," I said bitterly.

"And now, once again, you have survived."

"Yes, lucky me. I took my eye off them for one morning!"

"Off Barry and Sean?"

"Yes!" I blurted. "Barry and Sean, my mom, my dad, my little brother! Everybody I've ever loved! I hate love! It's a trap! I never want to love anybody or anything again!" The adult woman in me heard the hysteria, the unreasoning passion, the melodrama in these words, as if they came from someone else's mouth. I found myself standing naked in a store window with my deepest, rawest emotions on display.

Quickly I drew back. "I'm sorry, Father. I'm not myself. I'm sorry."

There was a long silence, and then the priest said, "Anne, when are you supposed to go back to your teaching job?"

I shuddered at the thought. *Eighth grade Latin students, overparented, bored, self-centered.* "My leave is up the week after next. They've got a nun subbing for me right now."

"Why not take the rest of the semester off?"

I shook my head reflexively. "I don't think I could do that."

"Why not? It's not the money, is it? Didn't Barry have insurance?"

"Yes, yes, I'm fine. It's not that."

"Anne, you're nowhere near ready to be around children again."

"But, Father, I have an obligation."

"Your first obligation is to make peace with God, Anne."

The words struck home, and I felt myself tearing up. "And how do you suggest I do that, Father?"

"Maybe a retreat would do you some good."

"A retreat?"

"There's a convent run by Benedictine nuns north of Grand Rapids."

"Wait!" I was aghast. "A convent!"

"Just for a month or so," he said gently. "It's beautiful there, Anne, quiet and peaceful."

"Peaceful," I repeated tonelessly. "A peaceful exile."

"Not exile, Anne, sanctuary. A place of safety where you can begin the healing process."

Sanctuary, I thought. *Peace and quiet. No demands. No need to put on a brave face.* A long silence ensued while I digested the idea and he waited.

Finally I sighed. "I guess I could try it for a few weeks."

"I'll make some calls," he said.

I passed up the holy water as I left the church. My thoughts came with cool detachment as I walked down the steps. *Get thee to a nunnery. So be it. Maybe I really don't belong here anymore.*

Interlude II

She stood on a grassy hillside. She was draped all in black, but I knew her by the lock of flame-colored hair that fell loose from under her palla. She stared down at two standing stones. There was no tomb, no monument, not even a shrine, yet I knew these were graves. I felt the aching hollow place inside her as she looked from the larger mound to the smaller one.

There were words on the newly carved stones that I could not make out, but I did recognize part of a date—August—and some strange numerals.

She reached out to drop a flower on the larger mound. It landed softly on the fresh dirt. Then she turned to the smaller grave, and she sank to her knees. I felt the emptiness gnawing, eating her from within. She did not weep. Instead, she began changing, slowly turning to stone.

Oh, Marc, she has lost a child!

Chapter 3

A simple wooden plaque was fixed on the high stone wall. "Our Lady of Prompt Succor," it said in brass letters. I drove through an apple orchard to get to the convent itself, and when I came around a little curve and saw the buildings for the first time, they looked just the way a convent should look, old, quiet, serene. The main chapel was neo-Gothic and sat atop a low hill surrounded by colonnaded, stone residential wings. On every side I saw growing things, flowers and apples and grapevines and blueberry bushes heavy with fruit.

My first sight of the nuns themselves wasn't what I'd expected. I'd heard the Benedictines were a conservative order, so the sight of women working around the grounds in jeans and tee-shirts seemed incongruous. But that was just for daytime. For dinner and for prayers, most wore a modified black and white, midlength habit. For Mass some of the older nuns still wore the wimple.

Life was simple and unadorned. There was a big, stone fireplace in the communal dining room but no decoration save the polished wood crucifixes on almost every wall. We had central heat but no air conditioning. On those first warm Indian summer nights, I lay in the dark listening to the crickets outside my open window. In other respects, though, the facilities were surprisingly modern, complete with wireless Internet. We were expected to observe "lights-out" after ten. I didn't mind. In the long hours of the night I came to prefer the rosy glow of candles to the harsh white glare of incandescent bulbs.

I spent most days working in the vegetable patches, weeding, pruning, picking. The pale, delicate hands that Barry used to admire became dry and freckled, and the bones jutted out sharply on my wrists. I knew the same was happening to my face, but it didn't matter. All my former vanities faded away. After evening vespers I'd sit and read in the rose garden. As the nights grew cooler, I'd wrap myself in a blanket and sit by the window reciting Hail Marys softly to the fireflies. I slept intermittently, rarely more than an hour at a time.

The nuns were kind and gracious to me, but they kept their distance for the most part, and I was grateful for that. One young nun, Sister Mary Therese, made an effort to befriend me, but I found myself covertly avoiding her. Something about her was too cheery, too eager. It made me uncomfortable. Soon she took the hint and backed away, greeting me with a smile in the corridor but no longer trying to engage me in light conversation. And, thank heaven, she stopped touching my arm when we did speak

When memories rushed up to plague me, I would slip away with my Bible or my rosary and sit beneath the shade of the apple trees, breathing the fragrant air and watching the play of light and dark green in the swaying branches above me. Gradually green became gold and then russet. The leaves spoke in a dry whisper as they shivered and began to fall. The sound of human voices, even the soft chant of prayers, had begun to annoy me, but it was quiet in the orchard. I was alone.

By October I had notified the school that I wasn't coming back, and the next day I went to Mother Superior and told her that I had been "called." She was skeptical, but I argued passionately. I told her I couldn't be close enough to God out there in the world with all its noise and distraction, that I found peace here, in communion with Creation, that I needed no other society but the sisterhood, no other love but Jesus. I became a postulate that November in a sweet, solemn ceremony in the old chapel.

Through the winter and into the spring, I told myself I was content. I seldom thought of Barry and Sean anymore. I was safe. Nothing could touch me. I believe I could have stayed there behind the sheltering walls of the convent forever if mother superior had not urged me to take on a Sunday school class in the local diocese. In some ways it was a good thing. I enjoyed seeing the children, hearing their little piping voices, and watching their wide, wondering eyes. They loved me, and the parents loved me, and the old priest praised my work.

But when the children came to me seeking love and approval, when they took my hands and clung to me, I felt something horrible rise up in me. A nameless dread, almost a kind of panic. Sometimes I had to consciously fight an impulse to push away from them, to shield myself. Afraid to confess this to the parish priest for fear he would think me unfit, I would flee to the solitude of the empty church and wait for inner quiet to return.

It was around that time that the first of the really virulent nightmares started. The boy in the boat. I woke up sobbing, crying out.

At first the sisters were all sympathy and comfort. They would rush in to wake me, bring cool compresses for my flushed and sweating face, sit up with me until they thought I was asleep. I would consciously slow my breathing and lie still until they softly closed the door, then I'd light a few candles and read from my Bible until daybreak. *It will pass,* I told myself. *This, too, shall pass.*

But the dreams didn't pass. They became steadily more sinister. A truly hideous one came the second week. It was similar to that first one I'd had back in Kalamazoo, but much worse.

I am in the chapel. Before me stands the main altar, but I am moving up the side aisle, toward the statue of the Virgin. I am carrying a basket of folded cloth to lay at her feet. I stop when I reach her and stoop to set my basket down.

When I stand back up, the statue has changed. Instead of painted plaster, she is made of white marble, with hair of brightest gold and lapis lazuli eyes. As she gazes down at me,

I realize, to my distress, that she is partially nude, with her breasts exposed and only a long drape covering her lower half. Even her pose has changed. The curve of her torso is languid, sensuous.

As I stare up at her in growing horror, I hear someone behind me, a woman's voice mumbling some kind of strange chant in a foreign tongue. I turn, but no one is there. "I don't belong here," I whisper, and the words reverberate off the stone walls altered and amplified as they come back at me. "Vu proprium hic non esse!"

"Shhhhh, Sister Anne. Shhhh, it's all right." It was Sister Mary Therese, leaning over my bed, her round, blue eyes full of concern.

"I'm sorry," I said, trying to reorient myself. "I'm sorry I woke you."

She patted my hand. "Don't worry, it's all right."

"Yes," I said weakly, "it's all right now."

She sat back and eyed me strangely. "Sister," she said, "my classical Latin is a little rusty, but it sounded like you were saying something like 'I don't belong here.' What were you dreaming about?"

I shook my head. How could I describe something like that? Something so surreal, so horrible, so grotesquely sacrilegious. "I don't know," I told her. "I can't remember."

"Well," she said, "never mind, it's over now. It was just a dream." She stroked my brow in a gesture that was meant to be soothing, but I wanted to shrink back. "Shall I sit with you for a while?" she asked me.

"No, Sister, thank you. I'll be fine now. I think I'll just read my Bible until I feel sleepy."

"All right," she said, and she got up. At the door she stopped and turned back, her eyes still troubled. "If you need anything, I'm right down the hall." Then she quietly closed the door.

But, it wasn't all right, and it wasn't over. It happened again on Sunday night, after I'd spent most of the day on a nature walk with my Sunday school class. I was exhausted and fell asleep after only a few minutes with my rosary.

I am in the middle of a crowd pushing its way down a narrow street in semidarkness. Bits of debris fall all around us, and I can't see where we are going. A man is speaking urgently to me, pulling on my arm. I have to get away from him. I need to go the other way, need to go back! But hands are clawing at me, people jostling and bumping, shouting as we surge forward. "Let me go!" I scream at the man. "I have to go back! Let me go! Sino mihi praecessi!"

"Sister Anne! Sister!"

"Sino mihi praecessi!" I grasped the hand that held my arm and yanked it loose, and the shock of actual physical contact snapped me back into consciousness. I opened my eyes and sat up, breathing hard, sweating.

Sister Mary Therese was standing there, rubbing her arm, staring down at me with real fear in her eyes. I saw Sisters Angelina and Justine hovering in the doorway. The two older nuns stood there in their nightgowns, their hair disheveled, their eyes wide and alarmed.

"She's all right," Mary Therese said, edging away. "Let's just leave her alone."

The other two looked at me dubiously, Sister Angelina twisting the belt of her robe, Sister Justine arching one brow the way she always did when something displeased her. Then the three of them backed out of the room, closing the door behind them.

Wait! I wanted to shout. *Don't leave me!* For the first time in so long, I felt an urge to reach out to other human beings. I was afraid, and I didn't want to be alone. But their doors were already closing, one after the other, down the hall. And what would I say to them if they did come back? *No,* the voice inside me chided, *they can't help you, and you know it.*

"Why?" I asked God. "Why is this happening?" But there was no answer. I lay in the darkness and said Our Fathers until dawn.

During the day, there were sympathetic gestures—a gentle smile, a reassuring pat on my shoulder. But as the weeks went by, sympathy turned to concern, then to worry. Smiles turned to wary glances from shadowy eyes that flicked away when I turned to meet them. Once I was a few minutes late for dinner, and I found my usual companions engaged in hushed conversation that ceased abruptly when I sat down. Then it was small talk and a forced cheerfulness carefully designed to avoid the obvious. They were becoming uncomfortable. I was becoming a problem.

Increasingly I kept to myself. I went to the orchard, but the summer heat was sultry and oppressive. I went to the library, but I couldn't concentrate on my reading. I sat on a stone bench in the garden and watched a coming storm roiling overhead, bending the roses to the ground, scattering the petals. Ultimately I retreated to my room, where I sat repeating the ritual prayers over and over. I told myself that in this way I was coping, that I was being a good nun, that this difficult time would eventually pass.

The worst dream came on a soft July night when I'd been more or less free of nightmares for almost a week.

It is night, and I am on a beach surrounded by strangers. They are all milling around frantically, screaming and running into the water. It is hard to see, and I am choking, and the sand is rocking and bucking beneath my feet. Then I catch sight of the one I have been searching for. My husband! He is running down the beach toward a small group of women who hold out their arms to him. I call out, but he can't hear me over the rumbling din.

The wind stiffens, and now sparks are flying all around me. Hot wind! Hot like a furnace! The stench of Hades in my nostrils ... burning, burning. Flesh cooking.

"Marc!" I scream. "Veni, Mar-ce! Festina!" He turns as he runs and casts me a last, desperate look before he disappears into the swirling darkness. A flying object strikes my forehead like a hammer. I feel it searing my flesh. From out of the blackness something huge and horrible is hurtling toward me. A scream struggles to escape my throat. "Mar ... M ... MaaaahhhhhAHHHHHHH ..."

"Sister Anne!"

Hands were holding me, shaking my shoulders. I was reaching up, clutching, fighting for breath!

"Sister Anne, wake up!" A splash of cold water in my face shocked me back to reality. I gasped, sputtered, and opened my eyes.

This time it was mother superior who stood over me. She was still holding the water glass in her hand. "Do you know where you are, Sister?" she asked me.

"Mother Superior!" I cried, stretching my hand out to her. "Help me!"

"I'm here, Anne," she said calmly as she pried my fingers from her sleeve. She sat down on the edge of my bed and began mopping the water off my brow with the hem of her bathrobe. "I'm sorry about your pillow," she said. "It seemed like the only way."

It was hard to lie still under her ministrations. I was still trembling, badly shaken, and my breath came in short gasps. My urge was to get up and run. Just run! Anywhere!

She had removed her bathrobe now and was lifting my head so she could place it over my damp pillow. Her soft cotton gown brushed my face as she stood up. "There, that should get you through the night. We'll get you a change of linens in the morning."

"Mother," I almost whimpered, "I don't understand."

"Shhhh, it's all right."

"No, it's not! It's not all right!"

"Calm yourself. Try to rest."

"But, Mother …!"

"No," she said firmly. "We can talk tomorrow. Just try to sleep now."

"I'm afraid, Mother! I'm afraid to sleep!" The borderline hysteria in my voice went bouncing off the walls and filled the room for a few moments.

She looked down at me with her quiet grey eyes. "Do you want me to pray with you?" she finally asked.

"Yes," I said softly.

She reached for the Bible on my night table and took it over to the straight-backed wooden chair by the window. Once seated, she opened it to Psalms and began, "The Lord is my shepherd, I shall not want …"

Interlude III

These are old, old visions. From back then, before you came home. I remember now. I was seeing her even then, Marc. She came to me in dreams. I was afraid of her. I thought she was a daemon.

Gods, woman, what are you saying?

Do you not see? These are not dreams. They are memories!

Whose memories, hers or yours?

Mine, but she is dreaming of them.

Then what were you dreaming of?

I was dreaming of her.

Forgive me, Daphne, but this makes no sense.

It is all coming back to me now, so clearly. His voice whispering in the dark ...

Chapter 4

"Mater, wake up! Come back!"

Small hands are shaking my shoulder. I open my eyes to darkness and turn to see the outline of my son's tousled head hovering over me. "Alexander," I murmur, "why are you up at this hour?"

"You were dreaming. I heard you trying to call out in your sleep."

I push myself to a sitting position on the bed and look around me. The covers are all over the floor, and I am dripping with sweat. I brush a damp lock of hair off my forehead. "Yes," I assure him, "it was just a dream, and it is gone now."

"Shall I stay with you for a while?"

"No, my heart, go back to bed. It was just a silly dream, and it is gone now."

He hesitates a moment then turns to leave. Before he can disappear through the drape, I call him back. "Alexander?"

He turns. "Yes, Mother?"

I reach out for him, and he is back in an instant, his light arms wrapped around my neck, his hand stroking my hair. What a good man he will be, both strong and gentle, like his father.

I wait until Alexander has gone back to his sleeping alcove, then I get up and pad barefoot out to the balcony that overlooks my street. The first hour is near. A hint of gray rims the horizon.

Torchlight spills onto the pavement from the bakery below. I can hear Paulus starting his ovens. The air is moist, heavy. Another hot day tomorrow. It is a long walk to the House of Vesta, but I will start early.

I sit on a stone bench in the shade of the temple peristyle and watch the high vestal's patrician profile as she turns to accept a cup of wine from her serving girl. She sips, unhurried, then swallows, and nods to the girl, who disappears like a shadow. The Virgin turns back to me and motions that I should drink.

Out of politeness, I lift my own cup to my lips and sip. The dark wine is so honeyed I can barely taste the grape. I set the cup down on a nearby table. When I look back up, the priestess sits regarding me with large, grave eyes. For just a moment, she looks like the goddess Vesta herself, with the morning sunshine filtering through her sheer white palla, wreathing her head in light. A fragrant breeze from the garden gently ruffles the dark brown curls on her forehead. I drop my eyes so as not to stare.

"So," she finally says, "tell me about this dream."

I gather myself, close my eyes, and try to recall it exactly. The images come back with a rush, sudden and vivid. I take a breath and begin.

"I was down at the harbor, standing on the sand watching a great white ship out in the bay as it headed in toward the port. I saw no sail, no row of oars, but it was coming in fast, slicing through the waves rather than bobbing atop them. As it drew closer, I could make out a figure standing on the deck, a woman dressed in white with her wild hair flaming against the blue of sea and sky.

"I cried out, 'Go back! Come no closer!'

"I turned to run for the safety of the town, but my feet could find no purchase in the sand. Looking back over my shoulder, I tried to scream at her. 'No, keep away!' But my voice was lost in the wind from the sea."

The virgin's low, precise voice cuts through my vision. "And then?"

I look up to find her eyes steady on me. "Then, I awoke."

She studies me for a long moment before asking, "Why do you want this woman to keep away?"

"Because she does not belong here!"

There is another pause while she takes a sip of wine then sets the cup down. "How many times have you dreamed of this woman?"

I take a breath to still the fluttering in my stomach. "Four times now, Lady."

"And you are sure you do not know her?"

"No, Lady. I have never seen her. She seems foreign somehow. From somewhere far away."

"What do you think she brings from far away?"

Doom. The word knots in my throat, but I swallow it.

"I fear she brings a sign of some evil to come," I say carefully. "Yet, at the same time I feel in some way connected to her, even after I wake up. She is telling me something, something very important, but I cannot hear her voice."

The vestal sighs and contemplates the paving stones for a few moments. Then she looks up and says something irrelevant. "Do you have a family?"

"I have a son. My husband is in Asia."

"They are well?

"I believe so."

"And you? Are you well?"

I shift on my cushions. It is uncomfortably warm out here, even in the shade. The priestess is waiting for an answer. With a sigh, I oblige her. "Perhaps a bit unsettled. Why?"

"Some say that dreams can give us glimpses into the future, and this may be so. But more often, I think, dreams give us a window into our inner selves."

I frown at her. "Are you saying that I do not understand myself?"

"Some parts of us are buried so deeply that we cannot know them when we are awake. We may feel uneasy but not understand why. That is when dreams can help us."

She sits placidly as I fidget with a stray lock that has come loose from my headpiece. Eventually she says, "Perhaps this woman you describe represents some piece of you that has gone astray, that feels lost. Is that possible?"

"Perhaps," I say to please her. Suddenly I am anxious to leave. I smooth the linen of my stola over my lap and search for the correct words.

Again she rescues me. "Who is your patron goddess?"

"Venus Aphrodite.

Now she leans forward, taking my hands in hers. "Then here is what you must do. Go to the Temple of Venus and make an offering. A blood sacrifice is best, perhaps a dove, but whatever thing is precious to you will do. Once she has accepted your sacrifice, ask her to clear your mind and give you peace. Then find a place to sit in the temple and wait. Do not think, simply wait. Wait until you feel the burden of your unease lift."

I stare at her for a moment then dip my head by way of thanks.

"You may come back," she says loftily, "should you have any more such dreams." Now she rises, and I do the same. The interview is over, and I have learned nothing.

I bow again. "You are most gracious, Lady."

The virgin turns without another word and strides off, the hem of her white robes billowing.

As I make my way down the curving colonnade toward the exit, I find myself more disturbed than ever. I had felt so honored to be granted an audience with the high vestal. I expected to be awed, inspired. And this is what I get? She tells me these dreams are creatures of my own psyche and sends me back to Aphrodite?

An attendant opens the big double doors onto the street, and I step out, blinking in the morning sun. For this I lost a whole morning at my loom? *Thank you, Lady, but I do not think I will be coming back.*

Chapter 5

Sister Angelina came to me after morning prayers to tell me mother superior wanted to see me in her private quarters. My stomach was queasy and my chest tight as I made my way down the long corridor. Mother answered the door herself and led me into her private library, where a tea tray was waiting.

"So, Anne," she began, dropping sugar cubes into her teacup, "tell me, what do you think is going on with these dreams?"

I was prepared, rational. "Well," I told her, "I think it must be my subconscious mind conjuring in my sleep what I won't let come to the surface in waking hours. First my parents and my brother, and then my husband and son …" I swallowed hard before going on. "I try not to let myself dwell on those things, but at night when I'm unguarded …" The quiver in my voice betrayed me, and I had to stop again.

Mother superior proffered a napkin, and I faked a light cough. Then I finished quite analytically. "It's got to be the unfiltered grief. At night it just seeps in and starts twisting things into evil shapes."

Mother sat, holding her tea, looking across the table at me. "I see," she said.

"Is that so hard to understand?"

She set her cup and saucer down. "Anne," she said, folding her hands on her lap and fixing me in her smoky gaze, "this is the fourth time this week. We heard you screaming all the way up and down the halls. And you were screaming in *Latin*."

"But, Mother, I was a Latin teacher. Don't you see? It's all tied to my previous life."

"Perhaps," she said steadily, "but you must realize how disturbing this is. Especially here."

"I'm sorry, Mother, truly I am. If I could make it stop, I surely would, but …"

She held up a hand to quiet me. "I do not want your apology, Anne. I want your happiness and well-being. I begin to fear that you will not find it here."

The hard knot of anxiety that had been seeding in my chest exploded outward, sizzling down my arms and into my face. She was throwing me out!

"Oh, Mother," I gasped, "don't say that. This is the only place I've known peace since my tragedy. I don't want to leave here." In my desperation, I tried to bargain with her. "Maybe it's just too soon for me to go out into the community. Couldn't someone else take the Sunday school class for a while?"

She reached out and placed her cool hand on mine. "Of course, my dear. That's not the problem. The problem is, hiding in here as you have been, you're not healing. It's been almost a year now since your husband and son passed on, and still you are not reconciled."

I stared at her. "Reconciled? How can anyone be reconciled to something like that?"

"By giving your grief to God," she said softly. "By finding your peace in him."

My outward calm cracked, and the heat rushed to my eyes. "But that's what I've been …!" My throat contracted, cutting me off. I rose suddenly and went to the window. Standing there gazing out at the orchards and the vines and the flowers, I clasped my hands across my stomach to stop them from trembling. I took a deep breath. "That's why I'm here," I said. "I'm looking for him here." Now I turned to face her. "Don't send me away, Mother, I beg you. The world is too much for me. My calling is here!"

She shook her head. "Your sanctuary is here, but I'm not sure it is a true calling. Some part of you is still resisting, is still angry."

I felt my heart jump. "Angry?" I said, and I heard the challenge in my voice. "With whom?"

She gave me a serene smile. "You know the answer to that."

"With *him?*" I took another tortured breath. "You think I'm angry with God?"

"I'm sorry, Anne, but until you've come to fully accept God's will, until you are ready to submit to it without question or reservation, you cannot be a nun."

"Mother!"

Now she got up and came to me at the window. She took my hands and held my eyes with hers. The aging skin of her face was translucent in the slanting sunlight. "Anne, I want you to take a leave of absence. I want you to go back out into the world and live. You're still a young woman, and you have plenty of time to make this decision. If you go and come back and still believe in your heart of hearts that you are meant to be a bride of Christ, then we will welcome you back and take you into the sisterhood. But today, standing here right now, I am not at all sure, and if you are honest, neither are you."

"Oh, Mother," I pleaded, "where would I go? What will I do?"

"Perhaps," she began carefully, "your dreams are meant to guide you."

I frowned. "Guide me? Guide me where?"

"To your salvation."

I stared back at her, dumbfounded.

"Think about it. What is the setting for these dreams?"

The answer was obvious, but something inside me balked.

"Anne," she prompted, "the dreams are in Latin. Classical Latin. Think. Where are you?"

Finally I said, "Ancient Rome."

"Yes."

"But, I've never even been to Italy."

"Exactly."

I just stood there, stiff, frozen.

"Come," she said, taking my arm and leading me toward a round book table over near the library shelves. She picked up a brochure and handed it to me. On the cover was a large, white cruise ship and the words "Ecumenical Tours."

I turned to her, astonished. "You want me to go on a cruise?"

She smiled. "Sister Angelina and I went a couple of years ago. It was wonderful, inspiring." She opened the booklet for me and pointed at the colorful pictures inside. "Look, it's not just a cruise. It stops at all the early Christian sites. Rome, the Catacombs and the Vatican, Naples, the ruins at Pompeii and Herculaneum …"

I felt a shiver up my backbone. "Herculaneum?" I whispered.

"Yes," she went on, "one of the resort towns on the Bay of Naples. It was destroyed along with Pompeii when Vesuvius erupted."

I just stood there staring blankly at the brochure, feeling lightheaded and queasy.

Mother superior's voice was saying, "Of course, it's entirely up to you, but I did take the liberty of inquiring, and there are still a few openings. You'd fly New York to Rome on August 18, spend two days there, then board the cruise ship for Naples. It docks at several ports along the bay, and there'll be bus tours to the historical sites."

I almost threw the booklet down. "But, Mother, I can't afford such a thing! I gave everything I had to the order when I became a postulate."

"Yes," she said calmly, "you came to us with a sizable dowry, and now we are giving it back.

"But all that money!" I protested.

"Don't worry about the money." Mother superior produced an envelope from her pocket and smiled as she held it out to me. "It has been earning interest all this time, and the archdiocese has authorized me to return the principle to you."

I drew out the check and stared at it. "But shouldn't this go to the poor? Shouldn't …"

She cut me off with a squeeze on my shoulder. "Anne, the sisterhood, as well as the parish, want you to go. We hope you will return to us, but if not, we want you to be healed, to be happy. Go, Sister. Go with a free heart and with our blessing."

I took up the booklet and stared at it bleakly.

"Trust me, Anne," she said gently, "it's for the best."

I had a momentary urge to drop to my knees and cling to the soft, dark folds of her habit. But I didn't do that. I just nodded and gave her the best smile I could muster before turning for the door.

The hollow tap of my shoes on the old wooden floors echoed behind me as I made my solitary way down the hall toward my room. In my hand was the rolled-up travel brochure. *All right*, I told myself grimly, *let's go to the source of the dreams. Root them out. Defeat them.*

Interlude IV

I was following her down a long corridor with many doors. A short white palla covered her head, and she wore strange shoes with hard soles that rapped and echoed on the wooden floorboards. She held something in her hand, some kind of scroll.

At the end of the corridor, a door was slowly opening, beckoning her toward … what? Beyond the door I saw only a dim horizon where stormy skies met an iron-gray sea. I tried to call out to her, to stop her, but she could not hear me, and the hard shoes were carrying her forward, into nothing.

She will fall, Marc. I know it! She will go over the edge!

Chapter 6

The ship's booming whistle broke through my daydream of Sean. We were at the school playground, on the swings, rehearsing what it would be like the first day of kindergarten. *"And I'll swing higher than anybody!"* he shouts, pushing off with his feet. His blond curls fly as he begins his upward arc …

A second resounding blast succeeded in shattering my bittersweet reverie. I opened one eye, squinting against the intense Mediterranean sun.

"Look, Anne! There it is, Naples!"

My new acquaintance Linda stood at the rail, her back to me. The wind splayed out her streaky blonde hair, making her head look huge over her sunburnt shoulders. "Geez," she said without turning, "it's kind of grubby looking, isn't it?"

I looked up from my chaise, momentarily annoyed at the intrusion. Linda was a nice young woman, pretty in a made-up sort of way, cheerful (almost to a fault), and reasonably intelligent, but she was a relentless talker. I'd begun to look for ways to avoid her on this cruise. But it was a small ship full of blue-haired retirees, and she'd rooted me out again.

"Are you going on the tour?" she asked me. "To Pompeii and Herculaneum? Guy and Larry are."

"I don't know," I hedged. "They're really expensive, and you only get a few minutes at each stop."

"Yeah, it's really a rip, but we don't have to take the cruise tour. Larry says there'll be all kinds of local buses and vans lined up at the docks. We can just pick one. They're a lot cheaper." She gave me one of her sly, questioning smiles. "Guy asked me if you were going."

She'd been trying to fix me up with one young gallant or another ever since we'd boarded the ship in Rome. All the way through the Catacombs she'd chattered on about her social life while I smiled politely and searched for inspiration in the ancient, sacred places. At the Coliseum she'd rounded up Guy and Larry, who'd joked and teased and pestered while I tried in vain to feel the suffering and the heroism of the martyred Christians who'd died there. The chatty threesome had even followed me to Vatican Square, and consequently all I remember of the place is their voices, laughing and talking, and the pigeons.

I lay back on my chaise and sighed. "I really don't know if I want to go badly enough to put up with Guy and Larry."

Linda leaned on the rail and regarded me with puckered exasperation. "I don't know what you have against Guy. I think he's adorable. And he seems to really like you."

"I have nothing against the man, Linda. He's nice looking, and he's very ... sociable, but he prattles incessantly, and he won't leave me alone for a second. That's just not what I came here for."

"Oh, Anne, don't be such a grinch!"

Grinch ... Dr. Seuss ... Sean holding up his book ....

I took a convulsive breath. Then I crossed out the image in my mind and looked up at her. "I'm sorry I'm not more fun, Linda. I know you're trying to include me, and I appreciate your good intentions. It's just that I like being alone with my own thoughts sometimes. Is that so strange?"

She stared at me through her sunglasses for a second then shrugged and turned back to the Bay of Naples.

I'd toyed with the idea of just telling her I was a nun. That would certainly do the trick. But every time the words were almost on my lips I stopped myself. I'm not sure I can explain why. I suppose I found something liberating in this unaffiliated anonymity. I was just

Anne—not Mrs. McCarthy, not Sister Anne—just me, out here all by myself.

And, I must be honest, even though I had not sought the attention of men, even though I found it embarrassing, almost alarming, it was still a kind of exotic and guilty pleasure to be noticed and admired as a woman once again. From a distance, though. The very thought of actually being pursued, of being *touched* by Guy, or by anyone else, was repugnant. Even the occasional fleeting memory of Barry's embrace was quickly banned the moment it flicked across my mind. That part of me was dead. I had buried it on a hillside in Mount Olivet Cemetery.

A shadow fell over my eyelids, and I opened them to find Linda standing in my sun. She sat down on the end of my chaise and assumed a sisterly tone. "Look, Annie, I know we don't know each other all that well, but let me give you a little bit of advice, okay? You've got a real pretty face and a nice body, and I'd kill for that strawberry blonde hair. And you seem like a nice person, although you are kind of an introvert. But I think you might be pricing yourself out of the market with this hard-to-get thing. You know what I'm saying?"

"Linda, I'm not ..."

"No, wait a minute, don't get upset. What I mean is, well, guys just don't want to work that hard for it anymore. You make it too hard for them and they'll go chase somebody else. Take it from me. You got to meet them halfway, at least. You know, put on a little makeup, maybe get a new hairdo?"

"I like my hair fine just the way it is," I said stubbornly.

She got up and stood over me. "Look," she said, her patience wearing, "we've still got a little time. Why don't we go shopping in the arcade? They've got some cute swimsuits down there, and you need a hat. What do you say? You want to?"

"I don't know, Linda. I didn't bring a lot of money."

"Oh, for God's sake, I'll treat. I can't stand to see you sitting around on deck dressed like a Quaker!"

"Is there something wrong with my dress?" I asked her, frowning a little.

She stood, hands on hips, looking down at me. "There's nothing really wrong with it, Anne, it's just so conservative. Don't you ever wear anything but virginal white?"

"It's cool, it's comfortable," I said, looking down at my cotton shirtwaist.

"Crap, if I had a figure like that, I'd be sitting out here in the nude. Come on, you can at least keep me company while I shop."

Finally I sighed and roused myself. "Okay, I'll go shopping with you. But we've got to watch the time. We'll be docking at Naples soon."

⊕　⊕　⊕

Back in my cabin, I tossed the shopping bag containing my new straw hat on the bed then locked the door and stood for a moment listening to the blessed silence.

No, the voice inside me said, *this charade can't go on.*

Crossing the little room quickly, I went to the vanity outside my bathroom and poured a glass of water from the sink. Then I stood, examining my image in the mirror as I drank. I'd cut my famous red-gold hair in the convent, but it was growing out now, curling wantonly around my face. I wore no makeup, but the sunscreen lotion I'd applied this morning glossed my cheekbones, accentuated my slightly tilted green eyes. The truth was, I did look … available.

"You're a nun," I reminded myself severely. "A nun!"

I clapped the water glass down, turned, and pulled my suitcase off the luggage rack. Carrying it over to the bed, I snapped open the locks and looked down at my postulate's headpiece, neatly folded under the false bottom. Carefully I drew out the coif and veil and walked back to the mirror with it. I placed it on my head and stood for a few seconds gazing calmly at my reflection. I felt the subtle change in my posture as I resumed my nun's identity and realized how lax, how slouched I'd become. I stood up straight and regarded myself reprovingly.

But, no, I didn't like this Anne either, this stiff, self-righteous prig of a nun. I pulled at the coif, and the veil snagged as it came off, tangling itself in my curls. Annoyed, I tugged it loose. Then I stood back up to smooth my hair.

What I saw when I turned back to the mirror stunned me. For a fleeting instant a stranger stood there looking back at me. Not my face at all. Dark eyes—sensuous lips—a wilder, more abandoned expression!

I gasped, and the veil dropped from my hands as I jumped back. The water glass crashed into the sink and shattered.

It had only lasted a second, but it was enough. I felt dizzy, disoriented. I stared into the mirror, trying to re-create that face, but all I saw now was Anne McCarthy, eyes dilated, mouth agape, hands clutching pale cheeks. *Dear God*, I though wildly, *I'm losing my mind! I'm going insane!*

I stooped and retrieved my headpiece. Carefully I brushed away the few droplets of water from the fallen glass, and as I did this, I stole another glance in the mirror. It was just me, standing there holding my nun's veil. Calm began to return. *It's okay,* I assured myself, *it's gone.* I took a deep breath and looked at myself squarely. My dress, I now noticed, had caught the worst of it. It was all wet down the front and definitely needed changing.

I turned quickly away and walked back to the suitcase with my headpiece in my hands. I replaced it under the false bottom and smoothed the folds. Then I closed the case and snapped it shut.

On the closet rod next to the dresser drawers was my only sundress of sorts—white, like most of my clothes, but sleeveless and scoop-necked. Hurriedly I pulled off my damp shirtwaist and threw it on a chair, then I grabbed the sundress off its hanger and slipped it on. There on the bed was the hat Linda had talked me into buying. I drew it out of the bag and looked it over. It was a frivolous thing, wide-brimmed with an attached powder blue veil. *Shades of Scarlett O'Hara.*

I carried it over to the mirror and put it on. Gathering up the blue veil, I tied it in a loose bow under my chin and examined my reflection again. Peering out from under the brim, my face looked small and wan, like a child playing dress-up. I reached for a pair of Italian sunglasses and put those on, too. Hidden behind them, my eyes didn't look so frightened. Now, with both sunglasses and a hat, very little of my face was visible.

You look like you just had a facelift, my inner voice quipped.

I took off the sunglasses and dropped them into my canvas hobo bag and checked myself one last time. The purse, hanging there on my shoulder, looked large and ungainly. And the weight of it felt oppressive and burdensome. I wanted to be rid of it.

Free yourself, the voice whispered. *Shed the baggage.*

I carried it back to the bed and dumped out the contents. The first thing to go was my overstuffed wallet. I wouldn't need my cell phone or address book either. As I felt around for more dispensable items, my fingers found the onyx rosary mother superior had given me as a parting gift. Slowly I drew it out. It lay there in my hands, stark and severe, the black beads glinting in the light from the porthole. I considered putting it on.

A rosary on a bus tour? my voice chided. *Why not wear a string of garlic around your neck, too? Come on, Anne.*

Smiling at myself, I slipped the strand back in my bag. I pulled a few euros and my ship's ID out of my wallet and put them in my pocket. Then, dropping the wallet, phone, and other items back into my purse, I stuffed the whole bulging bag into my suitcase and snapped the lock. I straightened myself, put on my big hat, placed a pleasant smile on my face, and turned to go.

Interlude V

Marc, I was there! Just for a moment, but she saw me!

What do you propose to do, femina?

Somehow I must reach out to her.

Our time is gone. Hers is yet to come. By what right do we interfere?

Compassion. It is a Law unto itself. Is that not what your Jewish philosopher said?

We can feel compassion without breaking the Laws.

Everything evolves, Marcus, even the Laws.

Everything in its own time.

You were always more of a rule follower than I.

It is not possible, I tell you!

All things are possible, carus meus. Surely you know that.

I see no way.

I will find a way.

Bona fortuna, wife.

Chapter 7

Pompeii was a disappointment, I'm afraid. It had been stripped of most of its art treasures. Only a few faded murals (some of them embarrassingly explicit) remained, and these were half-hidden by scaffolds. A recent earthquake had so weakened the old walls that only a tiny portion of the ancient city was still open to the public. And into this cramped space our loud and irreverent tour group was disgorged from the bus, to be herded around for an hour, perspiring and complaining while the guide droned on.

I found myself longing to be alone in the place. I wanted to touch the old things that ancient hands had touched, hear the voices of the ancient ghosts. There had been a Christian underground here, brave men and women. Faith had been so real to these people, so dynamic, so tangible a force in their lives that they'd been willing to die for it. I felt, instinctively and profoundly, that what they'd lived and died for was still here someplace. I'd hoped that being here would rekindle something in me that I felt was missing—had been missing for some time now. The rapture, the thrill of certainty. It was here somewhere. Perhaps in these ancient stones ...

"Come on, Anne. The bus is leaving." It was Linda, tugging at my arm. "Come on, we've still got Herculaneum to see. Isn't this fun? Hurry up, Larry's saving us a seat."

Once we were all stuffed back onto the bus and seated, the chitchat began again. I sat by the open window, perspiring, my hair blowing around in the hot breeze, getting in my eyes. I reached for my big hat and was preparing to put it on when the bus hit a hard bump in the road. I lost hold of the hat, and it blew out the window, trailing behind us like a kite as I clutched the veil and tried to pull it back. Larry, sitting behind me, reached out and gave it a yank, and the veil came loose as the hat bounced off the side of the window and flew away.

"Hey, sorry about that," he said, shrugging.

I gave him a polite smile and tied the veil loosely under my chin to control my hair. Then I turned back to the window.

We were entering a sleepy-looking Italian town with narrow streets and overhanging balconies. Linda leaned over from her aisle seat and read from the guidebook. "Ercolano. Hmmm …" She peered past me out the window at the aging residential area we were passing. "Squalid little burg, isn't it?"

Guy stuck his cropped, beach-blond head over the seat. "Probably a corruption of the original name. You know, Ercolano? Herculaneum? Don't you think, Anne? I mean, you're up on this stuff."

"Yes," I said, "probably so."

Linda was still looking at the brochure. "Says here they still have earthquakes all the time. I bet they were having quakes before the big eruption, but people were sort of used to it, you know?"

"Yeah," Guy put in, "we have tremors all the time back in Malibu, right, Larry? I mean, nobody worries about it."

Larry grinned and sat back. "Livin' on the fault line, man. You don't even think about it after a while."

Guy's head reappeared over the seat. "You know, you girls ought to come out to the coast for a visit sometime. We'd like to show you around."

The bus lurched to a sudden stop, and our Italian tour guide stood up and turned to face us. He spoke with a pronounced accent, carefully, as if by rote: "Ladies and-a gentlemen, this is the ancient Roman city of Herculaneum. It was-a smaller than Pompeii and considered more beautiful. It was a popular resort town, and many Roman nobles had villas and pleasure boats here. It was also a wine-growing center and a shipping port. A small earthquake has recently exposed a new section of-a the old city, which you see below us on your right. An international team of archeologists are now excavating the new site. We have one hour to see the points of interest. Please-a stay together."

I looked out the window. We were parked in front of a grandiose archway sporting the greeting "Welcome to HERCULANEUM" in Latin-looking letters. It wasn't what I'd expected somehow. There was a disingenuous quality about the manicured walkway, the self-conscious classicism. Still, a strange sensation was brewing in my chest, a kind of tingle, like the butterflies I'd felt when I was seven and my parents took me to Disney World. I was sitting there with what must have been a rapt expression on my face when Linda called out, "Come on, Anne, get the lead out! Anne! Are you coming?"

I gathered myself, adjusted my veil, and climbed out of the bus.

Inside the entrance our guide was continuing his canned speech while handing out maps and brochures. I edged around the group and went directly to the tubular metal railing that encircled the partially revealed ancient city—a hole in the ground gashed out of the center of Ercolano's decaying residential district. Shimmering under the afternoon sun, I saw Herculaneum's grayed plaster walls, red-tiled roofs still in place here and there, narrow, paved streets running straight and regular in a rectangular grid, ragged grass and a few native trees growing in the abandoned courtyards and gardens. Now this, I thought, is real! People lived here! It pulled at me with a strange magnetic force unlike anything I'd felt at Pompeii. I felt almost giddy looking down at it.

We began moving off in a disorganized clump, following the elevated pathway that circled the excavation. I drifted along at the back of the group, gazing at the old streets and courtyards, imagining them as they had been, full of life and color ... white walls with red trim, awnings of green and blue and rich brown ... pedestrians strolling by in their tunics and togas.

The group stopped again, and our guide was pointing over the railing. "Just-a below us is the Decumanus Maximus. Number ten on-a your map. As you can see, it was a-wider than the other streets and was used mainly for parades and ceremonial …"

No, I thought, this was the main business district. There were shops and restaurants and apartments all along here. The Basilica was just down the street. A huge statue stood in front of it. And right below us should be the Forum. I leaned over, but where the Forum should be the excavation stopped. I felt dizzy, disoriented for a moment.

The tour was moving off again, and I followed until we came to a long walkway that skirted the southwest boundary of the ruins. At this point Herculaneum seemed to come to an abrupt stop. The ruins fell away to a deeper strip of barren earth that ran along what might have been the old city walls. Stone ramps led up to the two upper terraces where the ancient buildings were almost at eye level from this vantage.

I walked over to the railing at the edge of the pit and looked down. Directly below me, at the base of the excavation's mud wall, a group of people, presumably scientists, were working on what looked like a human skeleton! I crossed myself.

Linda's voice seemed to come from a long way off. "Come on, Anne! We're going down!"

I looked up to where she stood with Larry and Guy a few yards away. The group had started straggling down the access ramp to the lower level. I smiled absently and waved. "Yes," I called, "I'm coming!" Then I turned back to the pit.

"Okay, Anne, you stand there if you want, but I'm staying with the group. Annie!"

"You go ahead! I'll catch up. I just want to take my time."

She sighed. "Okay, but don't get lost. This guy isn't counting heads. You don't want to get stranded."

I didn't give Linda an answer, only a vague, distracted look. *Stranded*, I mused, odd word. Literally, left on the strand, or beach.

Linda was still standing with a hand on her hip when Larry muttered, "Come on," and took her elbow. She looked up at him then shrugged and turned to follow the group down the steps that descended into the ancient city. Finally fed up, Guy waved a dismissive hand at me and headed off after the others. I watched them disappear, and their voices were fading as I turned to lean over the railing again.

Down at the excavation site, a young man was carefully brushing off a partially revealed skeleton that protruded out of the dust. The man was dark, bearded, barely clothed in a cropped, sleeveless shirt and cut-off jeans. As I watched, he sat up and wiped his forehead with a red bandana he wore like an Indian headband.

I waited until I could no longer see either Linda or the rest of the tour group before I made my own way down the ramp and descended into the ancient city.

Interlude VI

It is very difficult, Marc. She feels my presence, but there is another voice. I do not know who it is or where it comes from. I think it does come from her world, though, not mine. It is harsh, critical. It chastises her every time she begins to feel anything. If she cannot tame this voice, it will leach out what courage she still has and leave her empty, like me.

You are not empty, Daphne. You are as passionate as ever.

But I lack a means to express it.

So do I.

Forgive me, Marcus. It has been a long time for both of us.

It has.

Am I becoming a stranger?

No, but you are becoming ever more impetuous when it comes to this woman.

Anne.

What?

That is her name. Anne.

An? You mean "Duck?"

I do not know what it means. It is just Anne.

Why would anyone name a child "An?"

Marcus, stop this. I am talking about the other voice.

Perhaps it is some other waterfowl.

Enough. I am through talking to you.

Chapter 8

The streets of Herculaneum were almost deserted. It was midafternoon by now, and few tourists braved the searing August heat at this time of day. The pale blue veil was my only sun protection, so I stuffed the ends under the shoulders of my dress and wore it like a hood over my head. Thus veiled, I walked the quiet streets undisturbed for what might have been an hour or more. I don't really know how long. I lost track of time altogether.

Many of the buildings seemed to have meaning for me. There was one in particular, a baker's shop with what appeared to be an apartment on the second floor above it. The door to the shop was barred, but an open counter faced the street. I could almost smell the fresh loaves on the shelf. On the wall was a hastily scribbled Latin graffito: "Janus Polibius needs your vote."

A doorway at the side opened on an old, rotting staircase, which I imagined led to the living quarters. I stood for some time looking through the iron grillwork barricade, wanting to climb those stairs. Why they drew me so I can't explain, but what I was feeling was a mixture of yearning and a vague, dull dread.

Finally I moved on, drifting in a kind of daze, down streets, under archways, up flights of steps. The sun hung low in the western sky by the time I came out on a wide, elevated terrace with a stone balustrade,

Facing the balustrade were the facades of once elegant villas. I stopped at a modern sign that read "House of Mosaics." It had been a wonderful mansion with murals on the walls and little alcoves and exquisite inlaid floors. A marble fountain had once graced the recessed pool of the atrium. I could almost hear it gurgling happily as I stood outside on the terrace and peered in. The beautiful mosaic floors had collapsed, and the entrance was barred, but I felt I knew this house. I knew where its doorways led. There were children here once. *Phantom voices echoing off the tile and marble, laughing and joking in Latin, ... the master's children ... the name Quintilius ...* I shook my head. I was feeling that odd, dizzy sensation again. I sighed and turned away, stepping back out onto the terrace.

And there before me was a vision of dazzling blue. *A sparkling bay under a vast, cloudless sky, a few small boats bobbing on the water.*

I blinked, pushed the veil away from my eyes, then looked again. The bay had vanished. Instead of sparkling water, there was only a steep wall of mud, rising to the level of Ercolano's greenhouses. In the distance was the new, modern museum that now housed most of Herculaneum's treasures. The actual bay was a good half mile beyond that. I was looking at the edge of the excavation pit.

But the water should have been there. Little fishing boats and yachts.

Calm down, I reasoned with myself. *You're tired and hot, and your imagination is running wild.*

I walked to the old balustrade and placed my hands on a section of stone railing that still guarded the terrace. As soon as my fingers touched the stone, I drew them back. *Hot! Hot and vibrating!*

I stood, puzzled and suddenly frightened, staring at my hands. They were uninjured, but they were shaking. I took a deep breath and reached out again to touch the ancient stone. This time it was cool and solid enough, but I only left my fingers there for an instant. Something about the way it felt under my hand was unnatural. It felt *alive* somehow. Absurd, of course, but my hand still tingled.

I felt very alone standing there, my blue veil fluttering on a rising breeze. It suddenly occurred to me I had no idea where my tour group was.

"Hey!" It was a man's voice, calling in American English. "Hey, lady! Get away from that railing! What the hell do you think you're doing up there?"

The voice came from down below. I leaned forward enough to see a group of people, the scientists I'd noticed when I'd first arrived, standing at the base of the wall of mud, looking up at me. The one doing the yelling was the young man with the dark beard and the bandana. He was still shouting and waving his arm. "Don't move! Stay there! We'll come up and get you! Stay right there, okay?"

I smiled and waved, feeling foolish, like a miscreant child. What *did* I think I was doing anyway? I'd lost track of my tour. I'd been caught wandering around where I wasn't supposed to be. I'd interrupted the work of these scientists. And now I'd have to explain myself to this person.

I watched the man with the bandana climb a stone ramp down at the end and cross the plaza on the level below me. A few moments later he emerged from an arched opening farther down the terrace. He was younger than I'd thought. In fact, he looked more like an undergraduate PE major than a scientist. His expression as he strode toward me was a mixture of annoyance, amusement, and something else. Relief, maybe?

When he was still ten yards away, his face broke into a suntanned grin, and he said, "Boy, you really gave us a scare, you know that? It's after visiting hours, and when we saw you standing up here we thought you were going to jump or something." The grin widened. "Guess we're all getting a little morbid. We've been working on these skeletons for weeks."

He came to a stop in front of me and stuck out a dusty hand. "Mike DeMarco, National Geographic Society."

"Anne McCarthy," I said, and disengaged quickly.

He stood there with his head tilted, a bemused expression on his face.

"Skeletons …" I prompted.

"Yeah, we're finding a lot of bodies down there on the beach."

"The beach?" I turned and stared down at where the others were resuming their work.

"The Bay of Naples. Two thousand years ago that was the waterline right there." He nodded toward the dig. "You're standing on the old seawall."

I didn't say anything to this, just squinted down at the pit, and then at the wall of mud opposite them, and then off into the distance where a thin line of blue marked the actual coastline.

"So what happened? Lost your guide or something?" He leaned toward me. "Miss?"

"Oh," I said, "yes, I guess so. Wandered off, I'm afraid. I'm sorry I disturbed your work." He didn't answer, just stood there studying me. It was almost rude. "I certainly didn't mean to startle you," I added.

He laughed. It was more of a snort and a toss of the head. "You're American," he said. "Where you from?"

"Michigan."

His eyebrows flew up. "You're kidding! I'm doing my doctorate at U of M, Ann Arbor."

"Really," I said as I watched a woman scientist dust off a skeleton down on the old beach.

"So where'd you go to school?"

"School?"

"College."

"Oh. Michigan State."

"Well, that's not it."

Finally I looked up at him. "It?"

"I thought I might have seen you before someplace."

Good one, Casanova.

He hung his thumbs in the belt loops of his cutoffs and stood there examining me as though I were a lab specimen.

I had to admit, something about those eyes seemed vaguely familiar, that quizzical expression. As the moment hung, I offered, "Maybe I just have one of those hometown girl faces."

He shrugged dubiously. "Maybe."

I decided to change the subject. "So you're an archeologist?"

He took a quick glance at my ringless left hand then made a new stab at impressing me. "Anthropology and history. It's a cross disciplinary program, dual doctorate. This is part of my dissertation project: 'The Influence of Eastern Thought on First Century Roman Culture.'" He paused while his dark eyes watched me for a reaction.

When he got only a bland smile, he pulled off the bandana and wiped his forehead. Then he rubbed his fingertips through damp, spiky hair and let the scarf drop around his neck, an effect he probably thought looked dashing. "So," he finally went on, "how 'bout you? What're you doing over here? Just a tourist or what?"

"Yes," I told him, "just a wayward tourist."

He didn't speak, just stood there nodding, his brown arms bulging out of his sleeveless tee-shirt, his eyes fixed on me in a curious, speculative way.

I drew myself up stiffly. "I don't have a map, but I was reading the street names back there. I gather the Cardines ran down to the harbor, and the two Decumani were the crossing streets. The Maximus seems to be the main thoroughfare, but it's at the edge of the excavation. Are you planning to dig out the rest of the city eventually?"

He shrugged. "We'd love to, if the locals'd just take the hint and move out."

I turned and gazed out over the ruins behind us at the modern town beyond. Then I turned back. "There are some interesting inscriptions on the Basilica. Names of lawyers and judges, legal codes, dates."

His eyes widened a bit. "You read Latin?"

"I teach Latin," I said with dignity. "Or at least I used to."

"Ah," he said, as if this were somehow sage. There was something annoying about the overly casual posture, the premature familiarity, the too-smart, glinting eyes. I looked back at him.

For an awkward moment neither of us spoke.

I blinked first. Stepping to the railing, I pointed down at the intact tile roof of a large, square building situated on a promontory just below us. "So what's down there?"

He came up next to me and looked. "That big building there? That was the Suburban Baths."

"Suburban? Sounds pretty modern."

"They were, back then. Brand new, state of the art. Very posh."

The interior of the baths flashed before my eyes. *A small fountain under the skylight in the atrium, and a marble bust of Apollo ...*

Mike was still elaborating. "... used to go in there and spend the whole afternoon. They had everything, cold pools, warm pools, hot pools, steam rooms. There were even private tubs and couches for massage."

"Both genders?" That had come out more disapproving than I intended.

He nodded. "Actually, we do think these baths were unisex. Men and women might have come at different times." He turned around and pointed. "Now, look over there, in the middle of the old town. See that big oblong building? That was the Central Baths. Those were older and not as fancy, but the men and women had their own separate sides."

I looked.

"Not much left, is there?" he commented.

I squinted down at the battered collection of walls that once was the Central Baths. *Intricate black and white mosaic floors ... the sound of women's laughter ...*

"Well," he finally said, "since you're a fellow classicist, how'd you like to come down and see what we're doing?"

I turned to meet his gaze. "You mean, down there? On the beach?"

He raised his eyebrows temptingly. "I'll show you my skeletons." When I didn't respond, he added, "Unless you think that'll bother you."

I felt suddenly short of breath, but I kept my voice cool. "Not at all, that would be fascinating. Thank you, Mr. DeMarco, is it?"

"Mike," he corrected. "Come on, let's go see the ..."

His voice trailed off as I stood there motionless in the breeze, trying to bring back the Central Baths. The vision was gone, but the sensation of swimming in time lingered. I shook my head to clear it.

I looked at him. "I'm sorry, what did you say?"

"The Sacred Area."

"Oh," I said. "Yes, where is it?"

"It's down there, on the second level." He beckoned and swung away from me. I watched the loose swagger of his gait as he paced off down the terrace. *Overconfident*, I thought.

He stopped a few yards down and turned back to me. "You coming?"

Fighting down a strange reluctance, I stepped forward to join him. We went down a short flight of steps and came out on the cobbled street again. A few more paces and Mike brought us to a stop in front of a masonry archway.

I peered into the arched tunnel that cut through the thick wall of natural stone. It wasn't long, just a brief incline down to the next level. I could see the sunlight on the paving below.

"What's the matter?" he asked me.

"Is this the same tunnel I came through to get up here?"

He nodded. "There's one at the end of each Cardo, but this is the only one that's still usable."

I'd followed the other tourists through it on the way up with no problem, but now going back down filled me with a sick dread. It was so narrow and so dark! The walls looked slick, as if the stone were sweating. I felt nauseated.

"Don't worry," he assured me, "it's safe. This wall is solid rock."

I stood, bracing myself with my hand on the stone, aware that my legs were trembling. Despite the heat of the day, the air wafting up from inside the tunnel was cold.

Stop it! my voice hissed. *This is neurotic.*

Mike took a step down the ramp and offered me his hand.

Finally I collected myself. "All right," I murmured as I inched forward, "here we go."

Ignoring his hand, I pushed my veil back a bit and took a first tentative step. I felt myself teeter as my foot came down on the pebbled surface. A distant roaring sound vibrated in my ears.

Mike came back up and leaned close. "Hey," he said, examining my eyes, "you doin' okay?"

"I don't know," I admitted. "I feel a little woozy. The heat probably."

"Maybe this is a bad idea."

I blinked, took a deep breath, and shook my head. "No, I want to go down."

He frowned and gave me a skeptical look. "You sure?"

I nodded spasmodically and took another step.

"Careful now," he warned. "It's a little steep."

I was in the tunnel. I closed my eyes and stepped down, stepped down, stepped down, slowly and methodically. I'd almost reached the bottom when a wave of dizziness washed over me. I reached out blindly to steady myself on a portion of the wall.

"Doin' all right?" he asked me.

"Yes, yes," I panted. "Let's keep going."

"Okay, take it easy. Almost there." He grasped my elbow as we started down again.

I recoiled instantly. "Please, I can manage." As I struggled to free my arm, I felt my foot begin to slide. I felt Mike DeMarco's bare hands grab at me then catch me under the arms. There was a brief scramble, then we were in sunlight, and my face was resting against the decal on his tee-shirt, so close I could actually smell him! Dust, chewing gum, perspiration, and a hormonal musk so aggressive it almost made me sick.

I gasped and pushed myself away. "Sorry," I muttered as I bent to brush off the skirt of my dress.

"You could have just told me you were claustrophobic." When I looked up, his face was serious, but his eyes were faintly amused. "I thought you were going to pass out."

"I just slipped, that's all."

"It's okay."

"Anyway," I said, adjusting my veil, "thank you."

"My pleasure."

I turned to look around. We were standing on a square landing that led to a second ramp, which angled down the side of the ancient wall to the middle level. Directly below was a rectangular plaza boasting a statue of some toga'd dignitary. "So," I said primly, "the Sacred Area, I presume?"

He smiled. "No, that's just the terrace for the Suburban Baths.

Flowers and shrubbery ... a shallow, raised pool with colorful fish ...

"The statue is M. Nonius Balbus," Mike added, "the city's biggest philanthropist."

"Oh yes, I saw his name on the Basilica wall."

"He probably paid for the baths, as well as the terrace."

A young man, tall and athletic, greeting people in the garden ...

"The Sacred Area was over there," Mike said, pointing off to the right. "Come on, I'll show you."

I followed him down the long ramp, more at ease now that we were free of the tunnel's confines. At the bottom he led me through an open passageway between the city wall and a ruined building, then straight ahead through another arched walkway. Finally we came out on a broad plaza that formed a second-level terrace overlooking what once was the bay. Lining the ancient brick wall along the back stood what looked like a row of small temple alcoves, some with intact altars. *Torches ... a festival ...*

"This," Mike said, "is the Sacred Area." He strolled along beside me, continuing his travelogue as we walked down the length of the terrace. "These shrines probably weren't open for private rites. Most likely they were used for public ceremonies and celebrations."

"Why here?" I inquired. "Why not in the Forum, where the big temples were?"

"Oh, I'm sure they used that, too, but this is right here near the harbor. It'd be the first thing people saw when they landed here. You know, visitors, sailors, et cetera. Must have been kind of like a welcome center."

"Yes," I said distantly.

Standing quietly, our backs to the dark sea, facing the shrines. Slaves standing ready to light the braziers inside each alcove, their torches glowing soft gold in the blue darkness. A drum and cymbals. The crowd stirs. The priests and priestesses have emerged from the Temple of the Four

Gods. They proceed in solemn splendor down the marble steps holding their bronze torches aloft. Our patron Hercules leads them out, robes of red silk flowing on the breeze, golden circlet gleaming in the torchlight. One by one, the altar braziers are lit as each deity enters ...

"In fact," Mike was saying, "based on some fish bones and other artifacts found here, this may have been where they held the Vulcanalia the night before the eruption."

"Fish?"

"They sacrificed fish to Vulcan on August 23, as an annual appeasement."

"Why fish?"

He shrugged and favored me with another of his boyish grins. "I guess Vulcan couldn't get much seafood underground."

I smiled, but something about his flippant tone made me uneasy. It struck me as disrespectful, almost sacrilegious.

"In any case," he added, "apparently it didn't work."

I stopped and turned east, toward Vesuvius. "No, I guess not."

He must have sensed my discomfort because he changed tack abruptly. "You're standing in front of the shrine to Minerva. See her helmet?"

I paused to peer at the carving below the altar, and the scene blurred for a moment. *A priestess in purple robes, her back to us, gold bracelets flashing as she raises her arms before the altar ...*

DeMarco's hand touched my shoulder blade lightly. "You feeling okay? You want to keep going?"

"Oh yes, I'm fine. This is just so real!"

He nodded. "I know what you mean."

He ushered me on down the row until we came to a stop in front of the Suburban Baths. "I'd take you in there," he explained, "but it's closed right now for some repairs."

"It's okay, I have a good imagination."

He nodded toward an open passageway near the middle of the terrace. "Think you can handle one more ramp?"

I met his gaze. "Lead on."

"Okay, but watch your step."

I followed, allowing him to take my elbow this time as we made our cautious way down the last of the ramps leading from the seawall to the dusty pit where the rest of the archeologists were working.

When we got down to the beach, he motioned for me to follow him and paced off to the right where a group of workers were crouching over a shallow pit in the sand. One of the people, a fortyish woman in a baseball cap, looked up briefly and regarded me with eyes like jet beads. As she stood up, I caught a quick impression of thin brown legs under loose shorts and lean, muscled arms. The small, sharp eyes darted from DeMarco to me and then back to DeMarco. The glance she shot him was frankly cynical.

"How's it goin', Jan?" he asked her.

She pushed back the bill of her cap with a gloved wrist. "This one's a soldier," she said, pointing to a pile of bones and artifacts lying in the pit. "There's no armor, but he's got a military sword and these tools strapped to his back. He was facing the women, so he might have been trying to help evacuate them when the big blast came."

"This is Dr. Janice Goodman," DeMarco was saying to me. "She's in charge of the dig. And, I'm sorry, what was your last name again?"

I'd been only vaguely aware of this exchange, because something very strange was going on inside me. The emotion was so confusing yet so compelling I can hardly describe it. An anguish was building up inside, an incomprehensible sense of regret and loss. I was standing there with my mouth open, gaping down at the skeleton in stupefied silence, fighting a mad impulse to throw myself on top of that dead soldier lying in the dust.

DeMarco's hand was on my arm again. "Anne?" He shook me slightly. "Hey!"

I looked up, startled. "Oh," I said, "I'm sorry. What did you say?"

"We didn't get your last name."

"Oh. It's McCarthy. Anne McCarthy."

Dr. Goodman pulled off a glove and extended her hand. "How you doin'?"

I shook it briefly then returned my gaze to the skeleton. "This man was a soldier, you say?"

"Yeah," she answered, "see his sword here and his metal belt? He wasn't dressed for battle, so he was probably working on a construction project at the time. They put soldiers to work on that kind of stuff when they weren't fighting. You into archeology?"

"Roman history," I mumbled. My head was spinning, and I couldn't think.

"Ann's a Latin teacher," DeMarco added.

"Oh," said Dr. Goodman, her eyes flashing to his then back to me. "Okay," she said, shrugging, "just don't touch anything." And with that, she turned and paced off in the direction of another group of younger workers down the way who seemed to have made a new discovery. DeMarco started after her.

I'm not sure what happened next. My recollections are all blurred and melded with my emotions. I vaguely remember Mike DeMarco's voice.

"Hey, what are you doing? Hey, be careful there!"

I was on my knees, crouching beside the skeleton. I was stretching out my hand to touch the head.

"Careful, these things are delicate. I'd really rather you didn't …"

"Mar-ce …" I remember murmuring.

"Wait a minute!"

It was just the tip of my finger that touched the skull. So gently. My hand drew itself toward the bone almost against my will. I felt *heat. Heat,* the instant before the contact.

MAR-CE! VENI! FESTINA! Marcus is running up the beach toward the women. Now turning, motioning me toward the boat. Behind me, the boatman waving his arms, calling to me. No sound against the roar. MARC! Can't go without him. Boatman pushing off. Flying debris, cinders. The priestess, her arms raised to the gods, still standing on the terrace … falling now! Her body writhing as she falls. The women engulfed in darkness. Now Marcus too. The roar deafening! Hot! Hot black wind! The world falling! MAR—Maaahhhhhhhhhhh …!

Interlude VII

It has happened again! This time she was here with me!

> *Leave her alone, Daphne. Whoever this woman is, she needs to stay in her own time.*

She is not crossing over on purpose, Marcus.

> *I don't care how she is doing it, or even if she is doing it.*

What do you mean? Do you think I am imagining this?

> *I did not say that.*

Then say what you mean.

> *If she is a real person, and if she is somehow crossing these barriers, then I fault you for encouraging it.*

I am not encouraging …

> *You are. You are calling her, showing her things, tempting her with mysteries.*

Why would I do such a thing?

Because it entertains you.

You think I would put her through that horror just to entertain myself?

Perhaps, I do not know.

Perhaps not, Marcus. Perhaps you misjudge me, just as you misjudge her.

Oh, Daphne, I am just tired of hearing this. You were right the first time. She does not belong here.

Chapter 9

"That's enough mouth-to-mouth," someone said. "She's coming around now."

I was on the ground, and people were huddled around me, talking, some in English and some in Italian. I was gasping for breath and clutching upward, clinging to Marcus's sleeve.

No. I opened my eyes, blinked, shook my head. Not Marcus. I struggled to sit up.

The arms that had been supporting me now helped me to a sitting position. It was Mike DeMarco's hand patting my face. He was talking to me in a low voice that came from a distance. "Take it easy, just breathe."

I blinked stupidly at him and tried to place myself in time and space. I was sitting on the ground next to the skeleton of a Roman soldier. I looked down at the grinning skull and shuddered, and another wave of panic rose up tight and clenching in my chest. I was dizzy and nauseous, and spikes of pain stabbed through my temples.

DeMarco's spearmint breath was on my face. "Don't worry," he assured me. "We're going to get you a doctor, okay?" Then he looked up and called over my head. "Who's got a cell phone? My battery's dead."

"It's just heat exhaustion," said a woman's voice, which I dimly recognized as Jan Goodman's. "She's probably been out in the sun for hours. Somebody go get the cooler, and we'll make her an ice bag."

"I don't know," DeMarco argued, "that looked like some kind of seizure."

Dr. Goodman squatted next to me, her hiking boots in my line of vision. She pulled up my eyelids and examined my pupils briefly. "She'll be fine." Then to someone behind me: "Where the hell's that ice?"

"She was hallucinating," DeMarco said from my other side. "She was screaming in Latin, Jan."

"So she's a Latin teacher, isn't she? She's been walking around Herculaneum all day."

Someone clunked the plastic cooler down next to me and flipped the top open. Through my paralyzing headache, I perceived DeMarco removing his head scarf, unfolding it, dropping ice cubes into it, wrapping them inside, making a pack. Then he was lowering my limp torso back to the ground. "Here you go," he said to me. "Just try to relax now. You're okay." Then the cold ice pack was on my forehead, and someone shoved another one behind my neck, and I lay back and let the real world return piece by piece.

I was okay, was I? Yes, the pain did seem to be subsiding gradually. I was breathing. My initial fear had faded into vague confusion, disorientation, embarrassment. I shielded my eyes and squinted up at him. "What happened?"

DeMarco's dark eyes bore down at me. "Do you have a history of epilepsy?"

"No."

"Any recent head injuries?" Jan Goodman asked.

"No, why?"

"Because, you just touched that skull and went into some kind of fit, that's why."

"Yeah," DeMarco added, "you were thrashing around and screaming and calling somebody named Marcus, and then you just keeled over and collapsed on the ground."

"I'm sorry," I said feebly.

His faint smile was less than reassuring. "How you feeling now?"

I made a wincing effort to return his smile. "Much better, thank you. I'm sorry to be so much trouble." I was trying to sit up again.

"No," he told me, "stay down a little longer. You still look kind of pasty."

"You want a doctor?" Jan Goodman's voice sounded impatient, as though she were disgusted with me.

It hurt when I shook my head. "No thanks, I'll be fine." I hauled myself to a sitting position and took a gulp from the bottle of cold water she held out to me. "I would like to find my tour group though. Italic Tours. I'm sure they're wondering what's become of me."

"Oh, they're long gone," one of the men behind me volunteered. "Pulled out a couple of hours ago."

"But," I floundered, "my cruise ship …"

"That's probably gone, too, by now," Dr. Goodman said flatly. She stood up and looked down at me. "You're stranded, lady."

Stranded.

Mike DeMarco was supporting my back with his arm. "Don't worry. We'll see you get back okay. Think you can stand up?"

I drank some more water then nodded. He wrapped an arm around me, and leaning on his shoulder, I struggled to my feet. There I stood, wobbly and nauseated, aware that he was holding me up. My head throbbed, and my legs felt like cold spaghetti. I'd never felt that physically helpless before.

"I'll be back," I heard DeMarco say to his colleagues. "I'm gonna take her over to my place to lie down for a while. When she's a little more lucid, we can figure out what to do."

I heard some chuckling. "Sure, Mike, you do that."

"Yeah, take your time."

"Look," said Jan, "it's almost quitting time anyway. Why don't I take her back to my place and call the American consulate in Naples? They'll know what to do with her."

"Please," I protested, "I don't want to be a bother. If I could just use somebody's phone?"

"Come on," said DeMarco, "you can use the land line at my place. It's only a block away."

"Hold on!" I heard Dr. Goodman say sharply. "You're leaving the site?

"You said it was quitting time, Jan."

She looked at me with her bullet eyes, then back at him. "Can I talk to you for a minute?"

He stood there propping me up. "Can it wait till later?"

"Oh, hell yes, I wouldn't want to interfere with your social agenda."

They stared each other down for a few moments, then Goodman disengaged. "Fine," she snapped. "Go. We'll just pick up all your stuff for you."

Through my blurred gaze, I saw them exchange a sardonic glance as we moved off at a snail's pace.

I vaguely remember struggling up an incline, passing through an iron gate, walking unsteadily down a street of old buildings, and then up a flight of steps to a quiet upstairs room. I remember settling back on a plump sofa and closing my eyes.

⊕　⊕　⊕

When I awoke again, it was nearly sunset. I was breathing hard, my heart pounding. I'd been in the throes of a dream so jumbled and chaotic I could remember only impressions. *Pitch dark ... torches ... people running madly, all in the same direction. MARCUS! Pushing my way through the crowd. ALEXANDER!*

I sat up on the sofa and looked around, blinking in the dim light. It took a minute or so to get my bearings. The afternoon's events came back to me in a succession of disturbing flashes until I finally placed myself in what must be Mike DeMarco's apartment.

The first thing I noticed was that he was not a particularly good housekeeper. The place wasn't exactly dirty, just disorderly and unkempt. The main room was small and dank, its one attractive feature a wrought iron balcony that overlooked the narrow street below. The only sounds came from the evening traffic that honked and rumbled outside.

"Mr. DeMarco?" I called breathlessly. "Mike?" Nothing. He wasn't there.

I didn't want to be alone in this place. I wanted to go home. Then it occurred to me that I didn't know where home was anymore. I was adrift, lying on a sofa in some strange man's apartment. Any place had to be better than this. Everything here was different somehow. Not just the external surroundings. I mean, different inside me! Something was happening to me that I didn't like, that frightened me. Feelings, new and unbidden and uncontrollable. Strange sensations.

My forehead had begun to ache again, and I was rubbing it when the door latch began to rattle. I looked up, startled. The bolt clicked, and I drew in a sharp breath as something heavy thudded against the old wooden door. Then it creaked slowly open, and Mike DeMarco stepped into the room, grinning, a cardboard box full of groceries in his arms. "Hi!" he called out to me.

"Oh," I said, "hi!" And I really was glad to see him.

He turned and kicked the door shut then started toward the kitchenette with his burden. "So how you doin'? Did you get some rest?"

"Yes," I said with forced brightness. "I think I dozed off for a while."

"Good, that's good." He began unpacking some pasta, his back partly turned. "Now a little homemade Italian food, and you'll be feeling like yourself again."

Whoever that is, I thought. I watched him take a fresh-baked loaf of Italian bread out of the box and put it on the counter. "I didn't mean to be so much trouble," I said from the sofa. "I hope you didn't buy extra food on my account."

He ignored this. "I couldn't reach the consulate," he called out casually, "so I thought you could just spend the night here, and we'd try again in the morning."

I sat up. "Oh, that's way too much trouble! I wouldn't dream of imposing."

Now he turned to face me. "It's no trouble at all. In fact, it's kind of nice to have a guest. Somebody from home, you know?" He smiled and winked at me, and I considered being insulted, but it was just too much trouble. I was feeling a little woozy, and I sank back down on the sofa pillows.

His next question came casually as he put a head of lettuce in the old refrigerator. "So who's this Alexander guy?"

I turned my head and stared back at him.

Mike pulled a bottle of Chianti out of the box and reached for a corkscrew. "You were yelling for somebody named Alexander. I heard you when I was coming up the stairs. You got a boyfriend back in the States, or what?"

I couldn't just explain the truth. It was all too complicated, too bizarre. I could just imagine how it would sound to this man.

Crazy, my voice whispered, *it would sound crazy.*

At any rate, all I said was "No, I don't know anyone named Alexander. But I was having a very strange dream. I was searching for someone." I looked up and shrugged. "That's really all I remember."

He was pouring two glasses of wine at the counter. "Hmmm," he said, "that's pretty weird. You had that same tone of voice this afternoon at the dig. It doesn't even sound like you. It's kind of creepy."

"I'm sorry," I said. "You must think I'm possessed or something."

He came over with the wine glasses and handed me one. "Well, you're different, I'll say that." He grinned and plopped down on the sofa next to me. "So you don't have a boyfriend, then."

I smiled a little. "No, Mr. DeMarco. No boyfriend."

He frowned and tried to look severe. "Mike. Mr. DeMarco's my old man."

"All right, Mike. Sorry. You're certainly not an old man."

Cute, Anne.

His wry smile glittered over the rim of his glass. "I'm very bright for my age, though."

"And what age is that?" As soon as it came out of my mouth, I knew I'd been baited.

"Twenty-five."

"And already a PhD candidate." I lifted my own glass. "Impressive."

Shut up! You're making a fool of yourself!

"Yup, academic wunderkind. How about you?"

"Well," I said dryly, "I wouldn't exactly call myself a wonderchild."

"I meant …" His smile faltered, and I watched him try to collect himself. "I mean, how long have you been teaching?"

When I just sipped my wine and gave him back an amused stare, he cleared his throat and tried again. "I was just wondering …"

"I'm twenty-nine, Mike. Anything else?"

He sat back and laughed. "Sorry, I'm not usually this awkward with …"

"Women?"

"People."

I gave him an ironic smile and took another sip.

"Anyway, I think it's sexy."

I frowned. "What is?"

His eyebrow went up comically. "You know, the mysterious older woman."

I drew myself up on the couch and sat primly, holding my wine glass. "Look, Mike …" I began.

"No, no." He held up a hand. "Don't worry, you're not trapped in a pervert's apartment or anything. But, look, you're a beautiful woman. I'm sure you know that. You can't expect me not to notice."

"Well," I fumbled, "I wasn't expecting to be noticed." My face felt warm. I dropped my gaze and began studiously smoothing a wrinkle in my skirt.

A long second passed before I glanced up again. Mike's eyes had become serious. "I thought I was dreaming when I first saw you today."

"Careful what you dream about," I said cryptically.

His innocuous smile returned. "Anyway, just take it easy, okay? You're safe." He stood up. "I'm going to start dinner. Why don't you go out on the balcony and get some air. You might feel better."

"Can I help?"

"Nope, temperamental chef."

Glad for the respite, I got up and let myself out through the balcony doors. Standing at the railing with my wine, I watched a few straggling pedestrians pass by down on the street. The sun was setting, and the heat had relented somewhat. There was a light breeze. Aside from the occasional bicyclist or homebound shopkeeper, the town was quiet now.

A few minutes later Mike reappeared with plates, flatware, and paper napkins. He set them out carefully on a round, wrought iron table near the railing then came to stand next to me. "Dinner's cooking," he announced.

I was raising my glass for a sip when the concrete under my feet rocked and then jolted. For a brief moment the world seemed to pause. Skip a beat. Then move on.

"What was that?" I almost whispered.

He smiled at me in the amber light, his teeth white against the black scruff. "You mean that little tremor?"

I nodded.

"We've been getting them on and off for a couple of weeks." He shrugged. "The old mountain's restless."

I turned to look at Vesuvius. A thin ribbon of smoke wafted from its peak. "Is it still active?" I asked him.

"Basically dormant, but it rolls over in its sleep now and then."

I turned to him. "You don't think …?"

"That it'll erupt again? No, not without warning."

I looked over at him, unconvinced.

Mike leaned back against the railing and regarded me with twinkling nonchalance. "Don't worry, they have ways to gauge the buildup. If an eruption was imminent, we'd be evacuating right now."

I swallowed and gazed at the mountain.

He reached over and tapped my arm. "Trust me."

I nodded and sipped.

He downed the contents of his own glass. "You hungry?"

"Sure, what are we having?"

"Spaghetti di frittata!" he called out, waving his hand in an Italian gesture as he walked back into the apartment and turned toward the kitchen.

If he was a bad housekeeper, at least he was a pretty good cook. The balcony ambience was explicitly Italian, with candles in bottles and chipped plates. The evening breeze was cool, and the crickets were out. I picked up a piece of melon from the fruit bowl and savored its cool sweetness.

"So," he said, dabbing his mouth with a paper napkin, "enough about me and my PhD. You probably find all this extremely boring. Thanks for listening."

"Not at all," I assured him. "It's fascinating work, and I think it's wonderful that you have your life up and running like this."

He gave a self-deprecating shrug. "Well, not quite yet. I don't exactly have a lot of experience on my resume."

"Somehow I doubt you're all that inexperienced." I looked down quickly.

Hussy! What's wrong with you?

When I looked back up, he was sitting there studying me. "So, no boyfriend. No husband, I trust?"

"No," I said slowly, "I'm a widow."

"Oh," he sat back in his chair, and his voice lowered. "I'm sorry. Recent?"

My gaze drifted over the balcony and wandered the rooftops. "It'll be a year on August 24th."

"That's the day after tomorrow!"

I nodded.

He exhaled deeply then leaned forward and laid his hand on the table near me. "Listen, we don't have to talk about it. I mean, unless you want to."

I shook my head. Talking about Barry with this man seemed very wrong somehow.

There was an awkward pause, then he asked, "Any kids?"

I drew in a deep breath. "I had a son. He died with my husband."

"Oh, God, I'm so sorry!" He seemed genuinely stricken.

I didn't respond, just gazed out at the treetops.

He was still for a long moment. I felt him watching me. "Is that why you're here?" he asked quietly. "To try and start over?"

I sighed. "In a way, I guess. A complete change." My gaze drifted off, and I shrugged. He didn't need to know the rest of it, the convent and the dreams and all that.

Mike's eyes were dark and serious as he watched me across the table. "I'm really sorry, Anne," he finally said. "I shouldn't have been prying like that. I just wanted to know a little more about you, that's all."

I reached out and touched his hand, which still lay on the table. "Mike, you've been nothing but kind to me, and I appreciate it. I know I've been a little difficult."

"No you haven't."

"Anyway, I want to thank you for letting me stay."

He shook his head. "No, really, it'll be great having you."

I gazed coolly back at him.

Mike flushed suddenly. He dropped his eyes and rubbed his forehead. "Shit, I can't seem to say anything right, can I?"

I was smiling softly as I gave his outstretched arm a little pat. "You must be tired. Why don't you go to bed? I think I'll sit out here for a little while longer."

"You'd rather be alone?" he asked me.

I nodded. "Just for a little while. It's been quite a day, and I need to collect my thoughts."

Mike stood up and stretched, and an enormous yawn escaped. "Well, I'm pretty beat, too, and I've got to get up early. I'll just clear this stuff away, and then I guess I'll turn in."

"No," I told him, "leave it. I'll pick this up and put it in the kitchen for tonight. In the morning I'll wash everything up."

"No, no," he protested, picking up a plate, "you don't have to …"

I took it away from him. "Mike," I said firmly, "it's the very least I can do. Really, I want to. Just go to bed. I'll be fine."

"You sure?"

"Absolutely."

He started for the balcony doors then turned back to me. "Look, Anne …"

"Good night, Mike. And thanks."

Finally he shrugged. "Okay. Well, good night, then."

He disappeared through the french doors, and I heard him rattling around in there for a while. Through the glass, I saw him making up the sofa with a pillow and blankets. At last I heard the soft creaking of springs as he settled into his old iron bed in the corner.

When I thought he might be asleep, I got up quietly and carried the dinner things to the kitchen, where I rinsed and stacked them neatly on the counter. There was a strange pleasure in it, this simple domestic chore. It reminded me of home, dinners back in our little condo in Kalamazoo, Barry helping clean up the kitchen. Then pleasure turned to pain. I finished up quickly and went back out to the balcony.

Standing at the iron railing, I watched a young Italian couple wander past. The woman was carrying a baby. My eyes followed them in the dim moonlight until they disappeared, ghost-like, down the street into the mist. Their voices floated back to me, the woman's soft laugh. I felt light-headed.

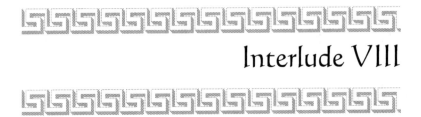

Interlude VIII

She sees, but she does not understand. It only frightens her.

Then what more can you do?

I must go back.

Back? Back there?

Back then. It is the only way.

Daphne, you will suffer it all again.

Yes.

Do not do it. I forbid you.

Husband, you can forbid me nothing. You know that.

Why must you disrupt our peace?

Peace! You call this peace?

It is what the Fates have decreed for us.

No. I do not accept this fate. Not for us and not for her.

You cannot go. If our son crosses the river and you are not here …

Beloved, he is not coming. He has moved on, and so must we.

So now it is we?

I must go, Marcus, and you must come with me.

Chapter 10

It is midafternoon, and I am standing on my wooden balcony overlooking the cobbled street below. My son Alexander has stopped to pet the street dog he has recently befriended. It is a brown, battle-scarred cur with one straight ear and one lopped one that falls roguishly over its eye. "Bellator," he calls it, after the gladiators. It comes around this time each day to beg for crumbs from the first-floor bakery under our apartment. Alexander strokes the dog's head and motions with his small hand for it to stay, then he disappears under the balcony. A moment later he emerges with a crust of bread and kneels on the stones to offer it to his wagging friend. Alexander sets his water bucket down and scratches the dog's ears. I see the pink tongue lapping his face.

"Alexander," I call down to him, "leave that dog alone and go get the water. I need it to fix dinner!"

Alexander grabs his bucket and jumps to his feet. He grins up at me, dark eyes and white teeth gleaming in a sun-bronzed face. Then he waves and, motioning to his canine companion, takes off running up the busy street toward the public fountain, the dog loping at his heels.

I sigh as I watch him go. Since earliest childhood, he's had this uncanny affinity for beasts of all kinds. I've never taken him to the games—indeed, I seldom go myself—but I know his distress would spoil the bloody spectacle for the throngs who enjoy that sort of thing.

My eyes follow him until he swerves around a slow-moving wine cart and disappears into the afternoon crowd. If the landlord had kept his promise to provide a water supply in the building, my child would not have to make these daily trips. But the fountain downstairs in our courtyard stands dry, as it has since the trembling under the earth began a month ago. I went to the public fountain the first few times, until I hurt my back lugging the bucket up the stairs. Now Alexander will not allow me to go. He insists that carrying water is not fit work for a woman. He is much like his father, even though Marcus has been gone since before our son was born.

Just as I am about to go back inside, I feel the boards under my feet shift and vibrate. Down on the street, there is a momentary pause, as if the people down there have skipped a collective heartbeat. Heads turn east, toward the mountain. The plume of gray smoke that billows from its cone is higher and thicker than it was yesterday. The gods are upset. Something is wrong in Hades.

⊕　⊕　⊕

A woman's high heels echoed in the darkness below me. I blinked and waited for the dizziness to subside. For a moment I didn't know where I was. I was gripping an iron railing, and it was night. Ercolano. I was standing on Mike DeMarco's balcony. But, where was the boy? Where was Alexander?

My God! I thought wildly. *What's happening to me?*

I pushed away from the railing and hurried back into the apartment, pulling the doors closed behind me. Mike had laid out one of his oversized shirts for me on the sofa. I tiptoed into the bathroom and changed quickly. Back in the living room, I laid my dress on the arm of the sofa, glancing over to make sure Mike was asleep over in the corner. Then I crawled under the blanket and lay there, faceup, staring at the ceiling, wishing I'd brought my rosary after all. The feel of it in my hands would have been a comfort.

Rough it, my voice said. *You don't need a rosary to pray.*

I settled back on the pillow, closed my eyes, and began. "Hail Mary full of grace the Lord is with thee, blessed art thou among women and blessed is the fruit of thy womb Jesus ..."   I'm   not sure how long I continued this whispered chant, but I must have fallen asleep around midnight.

⊕   ⊕   ⊕

"It is Alexander, the weaver's son! How are you today, my boy?" Julius Praxis claps Alexander twice on the shoulders then takes the stack of fabrics from the boy's arms and hands them to the seamstress. "Take Alexander back to the workroom and show him some of the new costumes we are making," Julius says to the woman. Then he turns back to me. "You do not mind, do you, Daphne? It will just take a few minutes."

I watch my son disappear through the draped archway that leads to the backstage area of the theater. "Not too long, Alexander!" I call after him.

Praxis puts a fatherly arm around my shoulders and walks me at a leisurely pace down a long passageway toward the stage area. He speaks to me in the deep, dulcet tones of the professional actor, and his Latin has the clipped, precise quality of a trained Roman orator. "Daphne, let me reason with you. We wish only to offer your son a priceless opportunity—a chance to better himself, learn a craft that could one day take him to the imperial palace itself!"

When I hesitate he goes on, gesturing extravagantly. "Why would you want to deny the child such a chance? Would you rather he grew up to be a weaver like yourself? Working from dawn to dusk in a stuffy back room, struggling to pay the rent? My slaves live better lives than that. Or perhaps you would prefer he join the military like his father? How long has Marcus been stationed in Jerusalem now? Eight years? What kind of a life is that for a man with a family?

"Daphne," he continues as we walk across the stage, "your son can have something better! He has all the gifts we look for—a graceful athletic body, expressive hands, a rounded resonant voice for a child. And those eyes could melt stone!"

"Yes," I remark, "he favors my mother's Greek ancestors."

Praxis points his finger in the air. "Exactly, the world's greatest actors!"

I smile but do not answer.

Now he stops abruptly and takes my shoulders. "Give him to me for a year, and I will make him the envy of the gods!"

I pull back, shaking my head. "He is too young, sir. He is only eight years old. He is very intelligent, but he still needs a mother's care. Perhaps when he is twelve."

"By then his voice may be changing. Daphne, we have an opportunity for him now! A friend of mine has a boys' choir, and they're set to sing for the emperor's visit this fall. We won't have much time, but I believe, with the right tutelage and intensive work, Alexander could be ready to perform—perhaps even as a soloist! He would be a sensation! Think of it, Daphne—your son performing for the emperor himself!"

I think about it and shudder inwardly. It is still too soon to know what kind of man this new emperor is, but the imperial taste for beautiful boys is common knowledge. "Yes," I say carefully, "well, I will have to consider it. It is a very big decision, after all. We can talk again when I come back later this week."

Praxis is opening his mouth for another reply when I look up and catch sight of my son talking on the other side of the stage with one of the theater's more notorious comic actors. "Alexander!" I call out. "Alexander, we are going!"

We leave the theater by the side exit and walk up the Decumanus Maximus toward the marketplace. The morning is unusually warm, and I would like to push the gauzy palla back off my head to feel the sun on my hair, but, of course, that would not be seemly. Still, there is a light breeze on my face, and I feel happier than usual today as we stroll up the sidewalk past the fruit markets and hot food stands. The rich smell of fish sauce wafts from the big earthenware jars in Graius's taverna, and I am tempted, but we have errands.

Herculaneum has made much progress this year. The Maximus has been repaved with fresh-hewn cobbles, and our new monumental statue of Hercules is a matter of much civic pride. There it stands at the main intersection, its richly painted surface brilliant in the sunlight. Up ahead I can see the great bronze horses and chariot atop the Basilica's pediment and, farther on, at the end of the street, the Forum arch rising white and majestic against the cloudless blue sky. Alexander and I stop at the curb and wait for a freight wagon to rumble past before crossing the street to the wool merchant's shop.

Alexander tugs on my sleeve, "Mother, can we go down there?"

I look at him. His gaze is fixed on the municipal athletic complex, down near the Forum. "The Palaestra? Why?"

"Something is happening there," he says, pointing. "Look!"

Even from this distance, I can see some kind of excitement at the end of the street. People are streaming toward the main building's columned entrance. "The stone throwing contest?" I speculate. "I thought that was tomorrow."

"Let's go see. Can we, Mother?"

By the time we get to the broad, paved square at the base of the building's wide portico, we are in the midst of a crowd. I stop a passing woman, grabbing her arm. "What is happening?"

"Soldiers!" she shouts back at me. "The fleet is just in from Judea!"

"Judea?" I gasp. "What legion?"

"The Sixth!"

Inside the complex, the playing field is ablaze with the glint of bronze armor. Soldiers are congregating in the yard, not in formation but mingling with the civilians. Women are rushing into the crowd to embrace some of the soldiers, and a few of the men are standing at the edges, apparently looking for loved ones. The men look dirty and tired.

My eyes begin frantically searching for the face I want. "Marcus!" I yell into the milling throng. "Marcus Fabius!" I catch a soldier by the leather bracer on his forearm. "Marcus Fabius!" I say into his face. "Is he with you? I am his wife! Marcus Fabius!"

The man grins down at me—a wide, gap-toothed grin. "Marc? Aye, he's here." He looks past me, over my head. "Fabius!" he bellows.

"Over here!" And then back to me. "There he is, mistress, over by the pillars." He points, and I turn.

And there he stands, centurion's helmet under his arm, eyes scanning the crowd. I hardly recognize him at first, so much has he changed. He is bearded, and the dark hair is long and shaggy on his brown neck. He has aged terribly under the merciless Eastern sun, but it is Marcus. It is my husband!

"Marc!" I scream, "Marcus!" Then his eyes find me. The grin spreads slowly across his face as he starts forward. I grab Alexander and run across the grass, dodging around people, fighting my way toward him. And then his strong, bare arms are reaching for me, pulling me close. I hurl myself against him, wrapping my arms around his neck, letting the feel, the smell, the heaviness of him sink in. He is here! Sea salt and perspiration and body heat. He is here! Right here! Hard leather and taut skin. My Marcus, home again! My fingers caressing his bearded face. His lips on mine, salty and wet and hot, pressing ...

⊕   ⊕   ⊕

"Anne! Anne!"

"Marc," I murmured.

"It's Mike, not Mark. Wake up!"

I opened my eyes to Mike DeMarco's face leaning over me, his mouth close to mine. My fingers clung to his hair, and I realized with a shock that I was about to kiss him!

"Oh, God!" I gasped. I wrenched my head sideways and pushed against his chest with all my strength. I felt short of breath, and my head was throbbing again. I could feel the sweat trickling down my temple. I struggled to a sitting position and pressed myself into the corner of the sofa, rubbing my forehead in confusion. Finally I looked up and found him sitting on the floor where I'd shoved him, staring incredulously at me.

"Oh, Mike," I said, "I'm so sorry."

"What in the hell is going on with you?" he asked me in a quiet voice.

I looked up and sought his eyes in the dimness. "I guess I was dreaming."

I felt his heavy sigh. "Boy, you must really have some wild dreams. I could have sworn you called me over here."

"I'm really sorry. I didn't know what I was doing."

"You have these dreams often?"

"Not this one," I hedged.

"It was that same voice again."

"Was it?" Now I was being deliberately disingenuous, and I could tell he knew it.

"It's pretty weird, you know."

"Yes," I admitted, "I suppose it is."

There was a long pause, and our breathing was the only sound.

At last I said, "I'm sorry I disturbed you, Marc. Please go back to bed."

"Mike," he said.

"Mike," I corrected. "Mike." I rubbed my aching head again. "I know your name, really. I just can't think straight right now. I'm sorry."

"Okay," he said, rising, "that's enough apologies for one night." He stood looking down at me for another moment. "You're sure you're all right?"

I nodded in the darkness. "Yes, thank you." Even to my own ear, my voice sounded feeble and unconvincing.

"Okay, then. Go back to sleep. I'll see you in the morning." He hesitated a moment longer then turned away and took himself back to his bed in the corner. I heard it creak gently as he burrowed down in the covers. Eventually, he began to snore sporadically.

I couldn't sleep, though. I lay there replaying the sensations. The balcony, the hot sun on my face, the boy smiling up at me. The theater's cool marble interior and the bustling street. Alexander's clear, piping voice. And Marcus. Marcus ...

Chapter 11

The Central Baths are on the Decumanus Inferior, only a few blocks from my home, and despite the midday heat, I am enjoying the walk—until I spot Dio the tailor sitting under the canopy in front of his shop. Aphrodite, I cannot be bothered with him today. I turn to step off the curb and cross the street.

But he has seen me. He stands and puts out a hand to stop me. "Daphne!"

"Sal-we, Dio," I greet him with a smile.

"When can I get that fine linen you promised me? The lady Calpurnia has ordered three new stolas and wants them right away."

"Soon, Dio" I assure him. "I am finishing the bolts for the theater this week. Then I will start on yours."

I start to walk off, and he calls after me, "Soon, then! Or I will have to find another vendor!"

I smile and wave. Tiresome man. His work is always urgent. Let him go elsewhere. I can only weave so fast. And now that Marcus is home …

The smells from the corner cook shop are irresistible. Sausages, fried fish, steamed greens, fresh nuts. I stop to buy a small honeyed fig cake and eat it while I walk. I am not usually so self-indulgent, but this is a special day. Marcus was called back to the ship last night, but he should be home for supper tonight. He is here! He is home! I can still hardly believe it.

I walk up the path to the Central Baths' colonnaded entrance with my bathing bag slung over my shoulder. Inside it rattle a comb, a flask of oil, my wooden strigel, and two thick towels of my own weave. The place is as familiar to me as my own sitting room. These baths are neither new nor elegant, at least not on the women's side. The frescoes are faded, and some of the tiles are missing from the mosaics, but the atmosphere is homey and welcoming.

I hand the doorkeeper a few coins and enter the anteroom, looking for the ladies I usually see there. Among the women sitting on the long stone benches sits Claudia Servinus, awaiting admission to the changing room. Her round face breaks into a wide, genuine smile when she sees me.

"Sal-we, Claudia!" I greet her.

"Daphne!" she cries. "Come sit by me."

Claudia is an ex-slave like me. Now she works as a barmaid at the inn, but you would never know it to look at her. Today she wears a saffron stola with a long, flowing palla of real silk. Elaborate jeweled earrings dangle from her ears, and her wrist jingles with gold bracelets. She probably takes private clients after work, but I choose not to concern myself with this. She is a jolly companion and good-hearted. I always enjoy seeing her.

I seat myself next to her on the bench, careful not to sit on her palla. "So, Claudia, you have not been to the baths for a week. You must be very dirty by now."

She waves dismissively. "Ah, I have been trying the new Suburban Baths. Have you been there?"

"I went a few times when they first opened. They are very fine and elegant, but I just did not feel comfortable there."

"Nor I." Claudia pouts her lip and blows out a puff of air in disgust. "Those rich ladies with their villas on the coast, they come in there in groups and occupy the pools for hours so nobody else can use them. And the staff will do nothing, no matter how many times you complain."

"Yes, I have heard that."

"I sat in the waiting room for two hours yesterday listening to those bitches in there laughing and squealing." She puffs again, and her voice rises. "You know, you cannot even get a rubdown without booking the girl days in advance? I have no time for that."

Here's my opening. "Nor I, especially today. Claudia …"

She cuts me off. "So?" She shakes her reddish curls and touches her earrings to make them dance. "What do you think?"

I duly admire her earrings. "They are beautiful."

"Lapis and carnelian set in gold."

"Are they new?"

"Yes, I got them for the Vulcanalia tonight. Are you going?"

"I do not know," I tell her with a smile. "It depends on what time Marcus gets home."

Her brow knits into a puzzled frown. "Marcus?"

My smile expands.

"Your husband?"

I nod, grinning.

Claudia's eyes widen. "Daphne!"

I lean over and grab her hands. "He is home, Claudia! He got back yesterday!"

She throws her arms around me and hugs so hard the pins in my hair come loose. "Oh, Daphne, how wonderful!" Then she sits back and looks at me. "Is it? Wonderful, I mean. After all this time?"

I flush slightly. "Oh, yes. But we really have not had much time alone together. He is still on duty for another week."

She smiles knowingly. "Ah, so you come to the baths to make yourself desirable. It is not necessary, you know. The man has been in the legion for eight years, Daphne. He would desire you if you had leprosy."

"I am sure he has had women, Claudia. Probably younger and prettier than me."

She pokes me with her elbow. "It is not the same."

I look down, smiling to myself, saying nothing.

Claudia takes the hairpins I am fumbling with and begins replacing them near my neckline. "Shall I do your hair for you after we bathe? I brought a bit of wine for a rinse."

I nod, still smiling. "If we have time."

Just then a stout female attendant steps forward and says, "Ladies, the tepidarium is free now. If you will step into the changing room?"

When Claudia and I have stripped off our garments and stowed them neatly in wall cubicles, I stop to wrap myself in a towel. She, however, simply drapes hers over her arm, turns, and starts to walk off. "Wait," I say to her, "your earrings and bracelets."

She turns and arches an eyebrow at me. "You think I would leave my new jewelry out here in the open? A bit of water won't hurt them." She turns back and struts, naked and bejeweled, through the archway to the warm room.

When we enter, Lydia Graius is already soaking in the pool. She peers up over the marble rim and waggles her fingers at us. Her husband owns the large hot food shop near the forum. He is much older than she and mistreats her when he's been drinking. Today there are purple bruises on her face and neck. I pity her, but what can anyone do? It is his legal right to beat her. Nevertheless, Lydia can be good company. She is quite funny in a wry, cynical way.

I undo my towel and ease my way into the warm water, but Claudia steps right to the edge, takes a deep breath, then immerses herself with a splash. She comes up shaking her hair and sputtering.

"Claudia," Lydia says in her Germanic accent, "By Juno, one day those jewels you will lose, wearing them in the pools."

"I like to be well-turned-out wherever I go," Claudia counters. She is full-breasted, and her fleshy orbs float like pontoons on the water.

Lydia snorts with distain. "Very frivolous." It sounds like "wery freewulus."

I turn to her. "Lydia, did you know Marcus is home?"

"So? When does this happen?"

"Yesterday. They let the men disembark here for the afternoon."

"Ah," she says with a crooked smile, "that will explain the commotion at the shop yesterday. Soldiers everywhere, tromping about, shouting, spilling the wine. Women all over them. I thought they are here for the festival tonight."

"My Marcus, Lydia! There he stood! I could hardly believe it!"

"And he is now where?" she inquires.

"They had to sail on to Micenum last night, but he is riding back this evening."

"Come, Lydia," Claudia puts in, "be happy for her!"

Lydia's smile warms a bit. "I am happy for you, Daphne. I hope he will now be good to you."

"Oh, he has always been good to me. He is a wonderful man."

Just then a deep grating sound reverberates through the room, and a sizable chunk of frescoed plaster comes crashing down onto the mosaic floor nearby. As we sit there, the water shivers, then ripples, then a few drops splash over the rim. Lydia has grown pale.

"Do not worry, Lydia," says Claudia, "these little shakings come and go."

Lydia shakes her head. "I do not like it, this."

Claudia raises an authoritative finger. "It is giants under the earth."

Lydia is twisting her yellow hair into a thick rope over her shoulder. "My husband, he blames Vesuvius." She snorts with contempt. "He is convinced the mountain is out to kill us all."

I look at Claudia, who is laughing, then back at Lydia. "But why? The mountain has protected us and provided for us for as long as anyone can remember. It is the home of Dionysus. Why would it turn on us now?"

Lydia drops her voice. "The priest at the temple of Apollo, he says it is those Christians who anger the gods."

"Aye," says Claudia, "I have heard that too. They were talking about it at the inn last night. Did you know that the city of Neopolis offered them a shrine for their god Jesus in the new forum, and they refused it?" She puffs through her lips like a horse. "Apparently their god is the only true one and cannot be defiled by associating with ours."

"I hear they are burning them in Rome," Lydia says darkly.

Claudia's eyebrows go up. "Who? The Christians?"

Lydia nods. "Men, women, children."

"Children?" I gasp.

"So I am told."

A terrible picture flashes in my mind. A child's hair burning. I throw up my hand to fend off this image. "Stop, Lydia! Do not say any more."

Lydia frowns. "Why not?

"I will have bad dreams."

She tilts her head and eyes me from across the pool. "Why? They are enemies of Rome."

"It is just horrid to think about, that is all."

Claudia jumps in. "Come, Lydia, you know what a tender little kitten our Daphne is." She flicks a few droplets of water at me with her thumb and finger. "Until something pricks that Greek temper of hers. Then our kitten turns into a tiger." She raises her hands and makes claws at me, and I have to smile.

There are a few moments of awkward silence as another tremor shakes the mosaic floors.

"Well," Lydia says in her driest tone, "I am hoping Vulcan can control those giants, because from their last brawl seventeen years ago this town is still rebuilding."

I loll back against the rim, my hair dangling in the scented water. "Yes, I remember it well. I was a young girl in the house of Lucius Quintilius. A handsome soldier came to rescue me when the balcony collapsed. He picked me up in his arms and carried me from the rubble."

Lydia's blue eyes have gone sharp. "So, Daphne," she drawls, "Marcus was already in the legion when you met him?"

"Yes, in his fourth year."

"But …" Claudia frowns as she puts it together. "I thought legionaries were not allowed to marry."

"Is forbidden," Lydia declares.

I smile at their transparent probing. "It is against the rules, generally. But when we learned I was pregnant, we went to old Master Lucius."

"Aha!" Claudia says.

I am suddenly on the defensive. "Lucius Quintilius was a good man and always favored me. It was he who sold my freedom to Marcus over his son's objections."

"And," Lydia adds shrewdly, "he is former legate."

I nod. "For the Sixth Legion."

"So," Claudia ventures, "he helped you?"

"Yes."

She slides me a smile. "And what did you have to give him in return?"

"Only a condition. We were allowed to marry secretly but legally. Then Marcus had to redeploy immediately to the Eastern front until his term was over. Eight years."

Claudia frowns. "So he never got to see his son?"

"No, Alexander was born two months after Marcus left for Jerusalem."

Even Lydia looks sympathetic. "Very sad for you."

"Yes, but at least my child had a name, and my husband had a reason to stay safe and come home to me."

We all fall quiet for a moment.

I decide to lighten the mood. "But now he is home," I continue, smiling. "And he still has the body of a young man."

Lydia rolls her eyes.

"No," I amend, "of a god. A big, bronze god!"

"Oh, please," Claudia says, "enough about Marcus maximus!"

"Ya, Daphne," Lydia adds, "if you are so hot, go sit in frigidarium."

I stand up to face them, water dripping from my nipples. "I cannot spare the time," I say grandly. "I must go home to my adoring husband."

They respond to my smugness with a cavalcade of splashes so ferocious the attendant comes over to restore decorum. I am laughing as the woman taps her staff on the mosaic tiles and bawls, "Enough, ladies! There is water all over the floor!"

What woke me was the pounding on the bathroom door.

"Anne! Anne, are you okay in there?"

I was naked and wet. I was standing in the tub in pitch darkness, ankle deep in cold water.

You're not okay, my voice whispered. *You're a lunatic!*

"Anne!"

"Yes." I stepped out of the tub, switched on the light, and looked around. Water was splashed all over the walls and fixtures. My white dress lay in a soggy heap in the middle of a large pool on the floor. "Yes, Mike," I called, "I'm all right."

"What are you doing in there in the middle of the night?"

"It was so hot. I couldn't sleep. I thought I'd cool off in the tub. I'm sorry I woke you."

There was a short pause. "Are you feeling better now?"

"Yes, I just want to rinse out my dress, then I'm coming right out."

"You sure?

"Yes, really."

"Okay," he finally said. "I guess I'll go back to bed."

"Yes, please do. I'm so sorry."

I listened for his footsteps on the wood floor, then the creak of springs on his bed. Poor man. I was driving him crazy.

I sopped up the water with a towel then did, in fact, rinse my dress out in the tub. Wringing it carefully, I realized just how pathetic I'd become. What reason I could still muster told me this had to stop. I had to get out of this place. I had to stop jerking Mike around. I had to leave. Time was running out.

But as I hung my dress over the towel bar, I found myself smiling while my mind replayed the sound of Claudia and Lydia laughing, splashing in the pool.

I never did get back to sleep.

Chapter 12

In the morning Mike was very polite. He was trying to be quiet, so I pretended to be asleep until he began opening cabinets in the kitchen.

"Morning," I ventured.

He looked up briefly. "Hey, how you feeling?"

"Much better," I assured him.

"That's good. You had a pretty rough night. I was going to let you sleep."

"Thank you" was all I could think of to say.

"Look," he said, sipping coffee from a mug, "the number for the American consulate is here on the counter." He held up a small piece of paper. "But you know, the Italic Tours bus comes through every afternoon about one o'clock, and I'm pretty sure you could hitch a ride back to Naples with them. Why don't you go for a walk, or just putz around the apartment this morning, and I'll take you back to Herculaneum after lunch?"

"Thanks," I said, "maybe I'll do that."

"Okay then, there's fresh bread and coffee here. I put out some clean towels in the bathroom if you want to take a shower. Just help yourself to whatever you want."

"You're very kind."

He smiled, a bit stiffly I thought, clapped his coffee cup down on the kitchen counter, and turned to go.

"Oh, Mike," I said, stopping him at the door.

"Yeah?"

"Is there a Catholic church within walking distance?"

He almost laughed. "There's one in every neighborhood. Nearest one's about two blocks down, on the corner."

I smiled at him. "Thanks, I think I'll go check it out."

He nodded. "See you around noon." Then the door clicked shut, and he was gone.

I sat propped up on the sofa for some time, gazing out the balcony doors. I couldn't blame Mike for being put off. My behavior had been nothing short of bizarre. I was bewildered myself. I'd never been like this before—secretive, irrational, even dishonest. None of it made sense. The decisions I was making at this point were inexplicable, even to me. They weren't even really conscious. I was on automatic, doing whatever blind instinct dictated. All I knew was that I couldn't leave Herculaneum, not now.

I looked at my surroundings in the morning light. I was in a man's apartment … a man I'd just met. It was unmistakably masculine. Untidy, randomly organized. Loose papers all over the desktop. Cups, glasses, dishes on the kitchen counter. Still, oddly, I felt at home here. Why should that be?

Shaking off this perplexing question, I got up and went over to the dining area, where my dress hung over the back of a chair. It was still damp. Shame crept over me as I held it in my hands, remembering last night's bathroom debacle. I could not, would not let anything like that happen again. I would have to get this Daphne thing under control.

I took the dress, found a hanger, and hung it on the molding over the open balcony doors to dry. Then I made up my sofa, smoothed the comforter on his bed, and cleaned the kitchen. Feeling a bit better, I went to the phone and called the cruise line. My ship, they told me, would be docking in Naples this evening; they would have the bursar pack up my things and leave them at their office for me. As for my return flight, I would have to contact the airline directly. Next I called Al Italia and told them that my departure would be delayed for a few days and that I'd be in touch.

What to tell poor Mike I didn't know. He was a perfectly nice man who had befriended me, tried to help me, and I was using him, manipulating him with innuendo and gesture and half-truths. Sometimes it didn't even feel like me doing these things. Sometimes this other woman, Daphne, seemed to be taking over my thoughts and emotions. I didn't like it. She had no right to intrude like this.

That's cra-a-a-zy, my voice whispered.

I am not crazy, I argued. I'm not. Stop it!

At least I was still sane enough to know that what I was doing to Mike was wrong. I didn't even try to excuse it. But I could not leave Herculaneum. Something here was pulling so hard on my psyche that I simply could not go. Maybe if I prayed for guidance.

I found the church without much trouble. It was a little chapel squeezed between an apartment building and a dilapidated house. I draped my sheer blue veil over my head and entered quietly. The interior was dim and smelled of incense. The only light came from two small stained-glass windows and a row of red votary candles along the wall. I crossed silently to the candles and lit one each for Barry and Sean, pausing to say a prayer for their souls. As I turned toward the altar, the room swam for a moment. There before the communion bench was a woman in a long white dress, her dark hair covered by a veil. She was standing, not kneeling, but her arms were raised in fervent prayer. Not wanting to disturb her, I took a seat on the side, a few pews back.

I bowed my head and reached instinctively for my missing rosary. More than ever, I wished I had it with me. Sighing, I pressed my fingers to my chest and tried to imagine its healing power. Then I began my soft recitation: "Holy Mary mother of God ..."

When my mind felt finally calm, I opened my eyes and looked up. The woman had gone, and I was alone in the church. I got up and began moving up the aisle toward the bench. There, looming above the altar, dimly lit by a small rose window, was Christ on the cross, his agony graphically carved in dark wood. I had never found this image disturbing before, but something about this one seemed strangely forbidding, almost gruesome. A few more steps and the beginnings of disorientation froze me. Even here this strange dizzying sickness could pursue me. Even in a church!

I stood, confused and frightened for a moment, trying to fight it, then I turned and hurried toward the exit doors

When Mike came back to collect me at noon, I told him what I'd done about the cruise and the airline. I finished with, "So, if you could just direct me to the nearest convent ..."

His brow creased. "Convent?"

"Yes, I'm sure there must be one around here someplace."

"I think there's one near Naples, but I'm not sure where exactly."

"Naples?"

He shrugged.

No, came my instant reaction. *Naples won't do.*

"Mike," I said carefully, "I know you've done so much already, and I hate to keep imposing, but ..."

He just stood there, watching me with troubled eyes.

"... but if you could possibly lend me enough money for a cheap hotel room in Ercolano? Just for a couple of nights." When he hesitated I went on quickly. "It's just that I left my purse on the ship. I don't have any credit cards or traveler's checks or anything." I fished in my pocket to show him. "All I have is a handful of euros and my ship's ID. I promise, I'll repay you as soon as I get back to Naples and get my luggage."

"Well," he said, shifting uncomfortably, "the thing is, I'm a little out-of-pocket myself. I'm not getting paid for this dig. In fact, I'm paying my own expenses with student loans. How much do you think a room would cost?"

"Oh, I don't know, I hadn't got that far. Look, if you haven't got it to spare, I completely understand. I'll just ..."

"Wait." He held up a hand. "I don't have much money, but I do have a sofa. You're welcome to stay here for a few more days if you want to." He gestured toward the threadbare couch and shrugged diffidently.

"Are you sure?" I said eagerly.

"I'm sure."

"Well then, thank you. That would be perfect. I'll try not to be too much trouble."

Mike nodded. "Great," he said, eyeing me a bit dubiously. "No problem." Then he brightened. "So, how 'bout some lunch?"

Mike walked me to the edge of the tourist-approved section of the excavation, but he informed me in definitive terms that the actual dig was strictly off-limits. Fishing in his pants pocket, he came out with a beat-up watch with an expandable band. Looped around the band was a key. "Look," he said as he slid the watch around my arm, "here's the spare key to my apartment, in case you get tired or you're not feeling well. If you're not here at five, I'll assume you left, and I'll go on home, okay?"

"Okay," I agreed, fingering the pouch.

He frowned down at me. "Think you can find your way back to my place?"

I nodded. "I think so. I paid attention."

"Okay, you know where to find me."

"I'll be fine."

I stood there on the seawall terrace and watched him begin his descent down the ramp to the dig.

I knew where I was going this time. In a few minutes I was standing under the balcony in front of the baker's shop. The stairs to that ancient apartment building beckoned me. The compulsion made no sense, but something was up there ... something ... I gripped the iron bars blocking the stairs and gave them a little shake. They seemed pretty solid, reinforced with metal brackets. I shook them again in a different place and felt a slight give, but it held. I gazed up the rickety staircase longingly. And my head began to spin.

Paulus looks over at me from the wooden plank where he is kneading bread. His eyes flick toward the new graffito crudely painted on his wall, and his dark, leathery face creases into a grimace. "Janus Polibius is a clown," he grunts. "A puppet for the rich wine merchants."

A small hand tugs at my arm. "Mater, can we take some cakes home? Can we?"

"Excusa-me," said a vaguely familiar male voice.

I came back from a long way off and didn't respond at first. "Excusa!"

I steeled myself, pulled the veil over my head, and turned to face the Italic Tours guide.

"Scusa, Missus, you cannot go there. The building is unstable." Then he took a good look at me. "I see you yesterday," he said accusingly, his practiced English lapsing. "You no get on-a the bus. Your friends, they say you are lost. We wait for thirty minutes, then we have to go." He scowled. "I get in trouble for leaving you here."

Now a group of tourists had gathered around the guide and were staring at me disapprovingly. A woman took my picture.

"I'm sorry," I told the man, "but I like to explore on my own, and I just lost track of the time. I'm fine, though. I have a friend to stay with here in Ercolano."

The guide nodded, still scowling. "You no coming back with us today?"

I shook my head.

"Hmmph," he said in disgust. "I tell-a the office I see you." And he walked away stiffly, followed by his flock of tourists. Good tourists, who stayed with the group.

I watched them disappear around the corner and waited until I could no longer hear the guide's canned speech and the tourists' babble. Then I turned back to the doorway to the staircase.

I laid my hand against the blackened wood.

It was *hot*, and it *trembled* under my palm! I jumped back.

Seized by a sudden, panicky fear, I backed away from the bars. *The seawall!* I thought wildly. *Get down to the harbor!* And I turned and ran, plunging down the old cobblestones in a headlong rush, driven by something huge and dark and menacing, something from my nightmares!

As I neared the first corner, a startlingly incongruous sight greeted me. The tour guide had stopped his little group in front

The Beach at Herculaneum

of a wine shop and was describing, inaccurately, how business was conducted there. I came skidding to a halt, bracing myself on the wall of a house. Guide and tourists turned, almost in unison, to stare at me. For an odd, disconcerting moment, I stared back. The guide shook his head then began gathering his little group to shepherd them forward. He cast me one last look over his shoulder before turning to usher a pair of elderly women off down the street. This time I read more alarm than disapproval on his face.

I stood there on the ancient street, my head reeling, the pain pressing on my temples like iron tongs. *No*, the rational part of my brain argued. *No.* I forced myself to breathe. *Get out of this place. Go!*

I don't know how I managed to find my way out of Herculaneum and back to Mike's apartment. I really don't remember much about it, just stumbling along on instinct, climbing stairs, falling onto the sofa ...

⊕   ⊕   ⊕

Alexander stands watching me where I sit at my loom. After a moment, he starts toward me. I feel him stop just behind my chair. His small hand touches my hair.

"Mother," my child says, and his voice is like a summer breeze.

"Yes?"

"When will father be back?"

"I do not know, Alexander."

"But will he be back for the festival?"

I turn on my stool. My son's soft, oval face glows in the afternoon sunlight, warm and golden and peached with a soft down that will one day become a beard. His eyes, gazing so earnestly into mine, are his father's, large and dark and lustrous, full of intelligence. What a beautiful child he is. What a handsome man he will become. "He has to ride all the way back from Micenum," I tell him gently. "It could take some time."

His eyes are growing moist. "But I told my friends he would be there tonight."

"I am sorry, loved one."

"I wanted them to meet him."

"I know."

He wipes away a tear forming in the corner of his eye. "Why did he have to leave again?"

I take his hands and smile into his eyes. "He will be back tonight, Alexander. He had to go pick up his belongings before the ship sails on to Rome. Next week he will ride back to get his wages and his discharge papers. Then he will never have to leave us again."

"And then he can stay here with us? They will not take him away anymore?"

My hand comes up to cup his face. "No, my heart, they will not take him away. We will buy a house with a courtyard, and maybe you can have a dog."

His face lights up. "Can I have the brown dog, Bellator?"

I smile. "Perhaps. We will talk to your father about it."

This seems to satisfy him at last, and he gives me one of his wide, Pan-like grins. "I want to go tell my friends. May I go?"

"All right, but be back before supper time."

"I will," he says as he turns to go.

"Before sunset, Alexander! Before the crowds start gathering."

He turns in the doorway. "Yes, Mother," he says dutifully. He stands studying me for a moment, then he comes back to my side. Softly he kisses my cheek. "Everything will be better for us now, will it not?"

I smile back at him. "Yes, my love, everything. Now go. Go see your friends and tell them the good news." As he opens the door, I add, "Be careful. Return soon."

He waves and disappears out the door. I hear his light footsteps down the stairs.

I sit for a few moments then get up and drift to the balcony door, where I stand and gaze down at my son's back as he runs down the street, his loose tunic flying out behind him. He looks so small against the panorama of the city. A trick of the light makes his hair turn golden for an instant, just before he blends into the crowd. Such a fragile life, so beautiful.

Then I hear a deep, rumbling sound coming from the east. I turn slowly. There in the distance, the mountain spews twin clouds of gray smoke high into the troubled sky, and the tongs of apprehension close around my heart. I turn back in the direction Alexander has gone, toward the harbor. "Come back soon," I whisper.

"Hey, there you are! What happened, you felt sick again?"

I spun around, fully expecting to see the drab walls and couches, my loom, my spinning wheel, my rolls of finished fabric. For a moment I thought it was Marcus standing there. But it wasn't. It was Mike DeMarco.

I was so confused for a few seconds that I really didn't know who or where I was. I blinked and didn't answer his greeting.

He swung the door shut and came over to where I was standing at the balcony doors. "What're you looking at down there? Anything interesting?"

Still disoriented, I just stood there, staring into Mike's face, so uncannily like Marcus's—younger, finer-featured, but the eyes, and the beard, and the dark, shaggy hair. I flashed on Marcus, standing there wearing a similar expression, smiling quizzically.

"Hey!" He was shaking my arm gently. "Anne! Hello?"

Finally I snapped out of it. Mike's face came back into focus, and I managed a smile. "Hi," I said with feigned lightness, "I didn't expect you so soon."

He showed me his wristwatch. "It's almost five. You hungry?"

"Oh, yes, of course," I said. "I'll fix it." I took a few steps toward the kitchen then wavered, rubbed my aching temples. Suddenly, my knees started to buckle, and I felt nauseous.

Mike's arms were around me, lifting me up, and then the room went black.

Chapter 13

When I came to, Mike was sitting on the sofa next to me, holding a cold cloth to my forehead. I drew in a sharp breath, and he sat back.

"Hey," he said, "how you doin'?"

My head was killing me, but I nodded weakly and tried to smile.

"Look, Anne," he began carefully, "I really think you ought to see a doctor."

I eyed him suspiciously. "What kind of doctor?"

"I don't know," he said with a shrug. "I just think we should rule out anything medical. I mean, this is not sunstroke, not after twenty-four hours. Look at you, you're pale as a ghost. It's not normal to be having these spells all the time. How often does this happen, anyway?"

I rubbed my aching temples. "It's never happened before, not like this. It's just since yesterday afternoon. I didn't sleep much last night. Maybe I'm just tired." I looked up hopefully.

He gave me a skeptical look. "Listen, I don't want to scare you or anything, but it could be, you know ... some kind of tumor."

"Please," I said impulsively, "just let me stay here a little longer. I don't want to get stuck in a hospital. Something's happening, and I need to find out ... I mean, there's something here that ..." I stopped and looked into his troubled eyes. "Oh, I don't know what I mean."

I put a hand on his arm. "But if you could just bear with me for one more day … please."

He stared down at me for a few more seconds, then his gaze slid away to scan restlessly. "Well, that's fine. I mean, I don't mind your staying here, but what if something happens to you? I might not be here, or even if I am, I might not know what to do. I'm getting a PhD, not an MD." His eyes found mine again. "I think you need a CAT scan or an MRI or something, but you'd probably have to go to Naples for that."

"Yes," I humored him, "you're probably right. But I'm flying back to New York in a couple of days, and I can see somebody there. Please," I touched his arm again. "Don't throw me out. Not now."

He sighed and regarded me for a few more seconds with genuine concern in his eyes, then he said, "Okay, I guess, but any more of these fainting spells and you're going straight to a hospital. Non-negotiable."

I smiled. "Thanks, Marc."

He frowned.

"Mike," I said quickly. "Sorry, slip of the tongue."

He shook his head, decisively. "Uh-uh, I'm not going for that anymore either. Who is this Mark, or Marcus, or whatever his name is?"

"He's … he was …"

"Yes?"

I took a deep breath. "Mike, you're a scientist. What do you think about the idea of reincarnation? I mean, do you think it could be real?"

He looked back at me, nonplussed. "Reincarnation?"

"I mean, do you think it's possible to, you know, remember lives you might have lived before?"

"Anne, this is getting wilder by the minute."

"I know, but please, just consider it with an open mind. Do you think it could be possible somehow?"

He shrugged. "Well, we always say nothing's impossible. But, as far as I know, it's just a bunch of anecdotes. There's no clinical evidence that proves anything like that. It's metaphysics, not physics."

"Yes," I said wearily, and I fell quiet.

"OK," he said, "let's consider it. You think you had a past life?"

I pushed myself to a sitting position on the couch. "Mike, I don't know how else to explain what I'm feeling … what I'm experiencing."

"Tell me about it." He sat there, his arm on the sofa back, gazing at me with narrowed eyes.

I gathered myself. The truth would probably drive him away completely, but at this point I knew I owed it to him. I took a deep breath and launched into my story. "This really started a few months ago, at the convent."

"Convent! You were in a convent?"

"Yes, back in Michigan."

He sat back. "Anne, are you telling me you're a *nun*?"

"A postulate. I hadn't taken my final vows."

"Jesus!"

"Don't blaspheme, Mike."

"Sorry, but you didn't think to mention this?"

"I thought it might make you uncomfortable."

He blew out his breath and got up. I watched him walk the few paces to the balcony doors and stop there, hands in his pockets, his back to me. I said nothing, just let him work it through in his mind. When he finally did turn around, a slow burn crackled in his eyes. "Okay, so why'd you leave the convent?"

"I got kicked out," I told him bluntly. "It was the dreams."

"The dreams. You mean, like last night?"

"Yes."

"Talking in your sleep?"

"Screaming, really. Waking everybody up. They took it as a sign that I wasn't at peace with God, and they sent me on this cruise."

"Wait, the nuns sent you on a cruise?"

"They didn't pay for it or anything, but they made it clear they wanted me to go. They practically shoved me out the door."

He stood motionless at the windows. "I'm sorry," he said quietly. "That must have been hard on you." Now he walked the few steps over to an old armchair opposite me and plopped down, elbows on knees. "So you want to tell me about these dreams?"

I told him. I told him everything, about the boy and the boat and the trembling ground and the voice in the church and the people running in the darkness. Then I told him about the face in the mirror on the ship and the strange, frightening visions I'd had since arriving here. He listened quietly, and when I finished and fell silent, he got up again. I sat on the sofa and watched him pace back and forth across the little room for what might have been a minute or so.

Finally he said, "So, when you passed out down at the dig …?"

"I was there, Mike. I was experiencing the eruption. I was on the beach, and Marcus was running, trying to rescue some women down the way."

"And Marcus is?"

"My husband."

"Your husband who died?"

"No, my Roman husband, Marcus Fabius."

"O-kay," he said slowly, "and who is Alexander, then?"

"He was my son, mine and Marcus's."

Mike shook his head. "I don't know, Anne, this is pretty hard to accept. How do you know these aren't just fantasies?"

"Mike," I said firmly, "I am not insane. I thought I might be for a while, but I know now I'm not. These are not fantasies, they're memories. Daphne's memories."

"Daphne?"

"The woman who lived these things. I see them through her eyes."

He sat staring at me for several more seconds, then he looked away. "Whew!" he said softly. "It's a lot to swallow."

"I know."

Once more he got up and paced back across the room. "So this Daphne, you think she died in Herculaneum, or did she get out?"

I shook my head. "She was down there on the beach." I said quietly. "Hundreds of people were out there."

"The beach. You mean the excavation pit?"

I nodded.

"The skeleton you touched, that was …?"

"Marcus," I said, and a shudder crept up my spine between the shoulder blades. "He left me … her … he died and left her standing there." The tears threatened but did not come, and I just sat there staring at my cold, trembling hands.

Now Mike came to me, sat down, and put his arm around my shoulders. He laid his cheek against my temple, and I let myself lean against him and accept his embrace. That was what finally undid me.

The dam burst so suddenly that I had no time to hold it back. The flood rose up and overwhelmed all my carefully built walls. Helpless to stop it, I let it come. The great spasms of accumulated grief took me, broke me like a twig in a storm. It went on and on. I keened and wailed and fought for air between sobs, until my chest ached and my throat was raw. Eventually I subsided into shuddering gasps. When I finally lay still in his arms, I was limp, emptied.

"It's okay," he whispered against my hair. "It's okay, you're not alone."

I just lay against him and sniffed through my swollen nasal passages.

"Wait here," he told me, and he got up, leaving me to concentrate on taking deep breaths through my mouth.

A moment later he was handing me a wad of toilet tissue. I took it, and he sat back down beside me. "Look," he said quietly, "I don't understand any of this, but I want to believe you, and I want to help you."

I blew my nose. "How can you help me?"

"By trying to figure this out." He sat forward and laid his hand on the side of my face. "Between the two of us, maybe we can make some sense of all this."

I was still shaky and short of breath. I could only nod.

"Here," he said, lowering me to the pillow. He brushed his hand gently across my brow. "How's your head? Still hurt?"

"A little better," I told him, and I took a deep, halting breath.

"Close your eyes," he said. "Just lie back and try to relax." A moment later I felt his fingers against my temples, his thumbs massaging my forehead in a circular motion. His hands were calloused but surprisingly gentle and sensitive. And there was his scent again, earthy and real and somehow comforting. I breathed it in. The pain in my head began to subside, and I smiled with my eyes shut.

That's when he kissed me. It was just a soft kiss on the forehead, but he left his lips there, breathing on my hair. I opened my eyes lazily. They traveled slowly over his throat, the dark whiskers on his chin, the swell of his lower lip. His mouth left my forehead and slid down over the bridge of my nose until it stopped inches from mine. His eyes were dark and soft and heavy-lidded as they locked on me. Neither of us breathed.

For a mesmerizing moment, we both hung suspended. Then I reached up to touch the dark stubble on his chin. It was both coarse and soft under my fingertips. He stayed still as I ran my thumb over the curve of his lip, firm and moist and smooth. Then my arms were curling around his neck. I was lifting my mouth to his.

For an instant he seemed to hesitate, then the current that flowed between us caught him. He came to me in an exhale of emotion, like a man who'd been holding his breath under water. I lay back on the cushions, and Mike's body quivered slightly as it pressed into mine, light but strong. His lips were on my chin, my eyelids, my ears. His throat pulsed. His neck was salty on my tongue.

"Oh, God …" he breathed.

And the spell was broken.

I disengaged, shook my head. "I'm sorry," I said, avoiding his eyes.

"It's okay."

"I don't know what came over me."

"It's okay."

"My impulses are so erratic lately. And they come on so quickly, I can't seem to …"

"Anne, I've wanted to do that ever since I first saw you."

I looked up. "I know, but that was only yesterday!"

"It happens that way sometimes."

"Not to me."

He gave the hint of a shrug. "Not to me either, until now."

"Mike," I said, grasping for words, "please don't think … I'm not like that, really. I've never been with anyone but my husband. Barry, I mean. I don't believe in casual lovemaking."

"I don't know about you, but this is anything but casual."

I buried my face in my hands. "I'm so confused!"

"I know."

I looked up into his grave young face. It was hard to believe this man was a virtual stranger. I could have been gazing into those eyes all my life, they seemed so familiar to me. His features hid nothing. His thoughts, his emotions, were right there, clear and transparent. I knew him. With a jolt I realized that for the first time in a year I trusted someone. If I wasn't careful, I could learn to need someone.

Mike smiled and reached down to touch my forehead with the backs of his fingers. "How you feeling? Is your head better?"

I nodded, grateful for the change of subject.

"Think you could eat something?"

I suddenly realized my stomach was empty and gnawing. I nodded again.

"Well, what I was going to tell you when I came in was that there's a little bistro down the block. It's cheap, and the food's good. What do you think, you up to it?"

Washing my face with a cold cloth at the bathroom sink, I worked to compose myself. I wrung out the cloth and folded it meticulously before laying it on the side of the bowl. Then I took a deep breath and looked up into the mirror.

Prick tease, my inner voice said.

It was just a kiss, I argued. It's not a sin.

The face that looked back at me was flushed and puffy and rather unattractive. Not at all the cool, unreachable beauty I wanted to be. I wished I hadn't broken down in front of Mike. I wouldn't have had him see me like this.

I dampened the cloth again and held it over my eyes for a few seconds. He's too young, I thought suddenly. It would never work out.

Work OUT? my voice jeered. *What do you mean, work out? Don't be ridiculous!*

Still, as I turned to go, I felt as tingly as a high school virgin—cold hands, fluttery stomach—all the symptoms.

Chapter 14

The bistro was quaint and almost stereotypically Italian, red-checked tablecloths and all. I let Mike order for me and sat listening while he told me about today's discovery.

"So," he said, his eyes bright in the candlelight, "you know those boat chambers down at the end of the beach?"

I leaned on my elbows and tried to recall the brief glimpse I'd had of the excavation site. "You mean the archways under the seawall?"

"Yeah. Well, we finally got the doors pried open, and guess what we found. About twenty skeletons all tangled together. Some of them were lined up in a row, so they were probably soldiers. Oh, and they had a horse in there."

"A horse? In the boat chamber?"

"Yeah." Mike leaned forward to investigate the basket of fresh baked bread the waiter had just brought. "Somebody must have tried to save his old four-legged friend at the last minute."

Plato, I thought suddenly. *The horse was named Plato.*

"Boy," Mike went on, "it must have been gruesome in there at the end."

I shivered and picked up my wine glass, finished the contents in one gulp.

Mike looked over at me. "I'm sorry," he said, "I wasn't thinking. We can talk about something else."

"No," I told him, "I want to know. I need to know. Everything."

He refilled our glasses. "Well," he went on, a little more carefully now, "it would have started that morning with a series of tremors and ash in the air. The actual eruption happened around one in the afternoon, but the pyroclastic flow is what killed Herculaneum, and that didn't come until late that night. The lava came after that, but everybody would have been dead by then."

I frowned and stared blankly back at him.

"Okay," he said, "let's back up a little. Eruptions go in stages. First you get the tremors …"

When my eyes widened, he held up a hand. "And, no, tremors don't necessarily mean an eruption is imminent."

"Okay," I said, "go on."

"Next come the plumes of smoke spewing out the top."

"Okay."

"Then comes the actual eruption. The built-up pressure from below finally breaks through and sends up a huge column of steam, gas, and volcanic debris that forms a giant mushroom cloud on top."

I nodded.

"But," he continued, "as that pressure vents, it gradually weakens. The process can take hours."

"How many hours?"

He shrugged. "It varies, but Vesuvius took over ten."

"So that thing was actively erupting all that time?"

"Yup."

I was aghast. "But why didn't they …?"

"Why didn't they get out sooner?"

"Yes!"

"Well, at first the mushroom was blowing southwest, toward Pompeii, so they wouldn't have recognized it as an immediate threat to them. They all went down to the beach to watch. Some local vendors even set up refreshment stands."

"You're kidding!"

He shook his head. "Look, Vesuvius hadn't erupted in a thousand years. They had no idea what was happening."

"My God," I murmured.

"It would've got bad pretty fast, though," he went on. "That cloud would be blocking the sun, so it would have turned dark. Ash and pumice falling."

"But why would they stay there? Why wouldn't they just run?"

"The roads were impassable. They thought the navy would send ships to rescue them, and according to Pliny they tried, but the water was too rough. The ships couldn't get close enough."

"So they were trapped there on the beach."

He nodded. "Anyway, like I said, eventually the volcanic pressure can't support the column any more, and the whole thing collapses." He was demonstrating with his hands, complete with sound effects. "And all that stuff that was in the column comes whooshing down."

I let out a shuddering gasp. *A deafening roar, something monstrous hurtling toward me from out of the darkness ...!*

"Now," Mike was saying, "you've seen pictures of volcanoes, right? You know that huge, billowing cloud of what looks like gray smoke coming down the mountainside? That's the pyroclastic flow. A wall of superheated toxic gas and debris traveling at hurricane speed. It's much heavier than normal air, in spite of the heat, so anything in its path is instantly suffocated, scorched, burned."

The horror of it silenced me. I contemplated my wine. The deep red liquid glowed against the candle flame. It trembled slightly as I watched. "Tremors," I said softly.

"Yeah," he said, breaking off a hunk of bread, "that's how we found this new section we're working on. One night the mountain rumbled, and everything shook for a minute, and the next day a whole new section of Herculaneum was there."

I sipped my wine quietly and considered my next question. "How long ago?"

He gazed back at me quizzically.

"How long ago did that new section open up?"

He shrugged. "About a year ago. Why?"

"That's when the dreams started. Last summer."

"Wow" was all he said.

"But they've been getting more and more vivid since I've been here. They seem to be building up." I sipped then added, "Like magma."

He finished chewing and swallowed before he spoke. "Well," he finally said, "tomorrow is the anniversary. August 24, 79 C.E."

"Sean's birthday," I said softly. "The day he and his father died."

"Oh, Christ, Anne!"

"Mike, please."

He leaned one elbow on the table and rubbed his forehead. "Sorry, I forgot."

The waiter appeared and plopped two plates of some kind of pasta down in front of us. I rolled a forkful and smiled across at Mike.

"But, look," he said, holding his fork like a pointer, "maybe that's why ... I mean, maybe it's not reincarnation or anything like that."

"What do you mean?"

"Well, there is some science for this. It's controversial, but some researchers think the brain is like a transmitter. It's all electromagnetic circuitry, you know. And, if it can transmit, it can also receive." Now he was getting animated. "For example, have you ever been hearing a song in your head and then turned on the radio, and there it is?"

I nodded, attentive.

"Well, these scientists think that's your brain acting like a radio receiver, actually picking up a station."

"So, by that reasoning, these flashes I'm getting are really, what? Ancient brain waves?"

"Exactly. A kind of experiential download."

I considered this briefly, and then I said, "I don't know, it sounds more like New Age mysticism than science."

"Not so fast. Look, there was a catastrophe here. All those people died on the beach. And it was sudden, like that!" He snapped his fingers. "When that hot blast came, no one could have survived more than a few seconds. One moment their minds were working overtime, the next they were gone. So maybe some of those thoughts and the emotions that went with them didn't die. Maybe they got trapped here, just lingering in the atmosphere, and you've been tuned in to the right frequency, and you picked it up."

I shifted restlessly in my seat. "But what am I doing in this picture?

He opened his mouth to say something then stopped. I watched the thoughts speeding across his eyes.

"What?" I said.

"Wait," he said to the candle flame.

I sipped my wine and waited.

In a few moments he said, "There was a guy I knew in grad school, 'Weird John' we used to call him. He was actually a brilliant guy, a biophysics major. I talked to him a few times over coffee. He was working on this hypothesis about the effect of hyper-consciousness on brain wave frequencies. I remember him using the phrase, 'a wormhole in the space-time foam.'"

I just sat there and frowned back at him.

"It's quantum theory, something about a thing being able to exist in more than one place at the same time. Of course, he was talking about subatomic particles, not complex organisms like …"

"Mike, I'm getting a headache."

"Bear with me. This is relevant."

"How?"

"Well, part of his hypothesis, like I said, was about brain waves. He was trying to devise an experiment to show that extreme emotional states can send the frequencies out of the normal range, way high or way low."

"And that's what he meant by …?"

"Hyper-consciousness, yeah."

"Extreme emotional states …" I mulled.

"Like fear, or …"

"Grief."

"Yes."

The implications fired and darted in my head. "Could I be 'tuned-in' because of Barry and Sean?"

"It makes sense. I mean, the date, and the fact that you and this woman both lost a husband and a son, and you coming here just at the right time."

I nodded slowly. "Maybe. It sounds right, but …"

"But you don't buy it."

I stared into my wine glass and thought about it. Finally I looked up and said, "It just feels like there's something else. I feel like I'm supposed to do something. Reconcile with her somehow."

"Anne," he said slowly, "she's dead."

I waved my fork in irritation. "Yes, of course, I know she's dead. I'm not insane. But when I'm with her, her life seems so much more vivid … so much more real than …"

"Than real life?"

"Than my life."

"Why is that, do you think?"

"Because she lives in the now, all the time. She lets her emotions go; she doesn't hold anything back. She's not …"

"Repressed?"

I felt a twinge of anger flare and laid my fork down. "Under. Control," I said precisely.

He looked at me for a few seconds then raised his glass and drank.

"Sorry," I said quietly, "I didn't mean to snap."

"It's okay."

Finally I challenged him. "You think I *am* crazy, don't you?"

He hesitated for a moment; then he said, "No, I really don't."

"Then why can't you believe me?" I almost pleaded.

He tilted his head in a dubious shrug. "I've just never seen anything like this before." He contemplated his glass for a moment then picked it up. "But," he said as he swirled the wine, "I guess anything's possible." He took a healthy gulp and drained the glass.

"Look at all the parallels here," I went on. "Barry and Sean … Barry and Marcus … Marcus and Alexander … Sean and Alexander." Suddenly I looked up. "Alexander! Mike, they lost Alexander!"

He frowned, puzzled.

I felt the panic rising in my chest. "What happened to Alexander? I have no final visions of him except for ..." I paused with the wine glass in my hand as the image flashed inside my head.

"Except for what?" he prompted.

"The boy in the boat."

"Anne, what are you talking about?"

"My nightmare! I saw him."

"Saw who? Alexander?"

I nodded. "I thought it was Sean. The features were indistinct, and he was in a boat like my brother, but I knew it was my son. I guess my mind just read 'Sean,' but it must have been Alexander! He was in the boat, trying to get away."

"But," he said slowly, "it's not clear like the other visions."

"No, it's all blurred and distorted."

"Well, then ..."

My hand went involuntarily to my mouth. "Oh God, Mike, Daphne didn't know! She died not knowing what happened to him!"

"Well, if that's so, then maybe it was a blessing. Maybe it's better not to know."

"No, Mike, he was her child! Why wasn't she with him?"

"Maybe they got separated somehow."

"She would never have let him out of her sight! He was her son!"

"But, Daphne ..."

We both froze in our chairs and sat staring at each other. It wasn't just the words he'd spoken. His face, his expression, had changed for a moment. Even his voice was deeper, gruffer.

"What just happened?" Mike asked me.

"You looked so much like Marcus just then. You even sounded like him."

"No," he said decisively. "No, I'm not going there. It was just a slip of the tongue, power of suggestion."

"Okay," I said.

"I mean, there's no reason why I would have any connection to these people."

"You're here, where it happened," I reminded him. "You've made a career out of studying the event. You're digging them up out of the sand, for heaven's sake!"

"I'm an archeologist!" he almost yelled at me. "That doesn't mean I'm reliving some past life or anything!"

"Well, why couldn't you be picking them up, too? I mean, their brain waves?"

"I'm not the one passing out and talking to myself in the middle of the night!"

There was an odd moment of quiet in the bistro, and his voice seemed to hang in the air. "Mike," I said, "people are staring."

He gave the couple at the next table a nod and a weak smile then turned back. Elbows on the table, he closed his eyes and rubbed his forehead for a moment. Then he picked up the empty wine bottle, examined it, and set it back down. I watched him ruminate for several seconds, his fingernail picking at the damp label. Finally he looked up at me and said, "When I first met you, up there on the terrace yesterday, I did think I'd seen you before."

I nodded. "I thought you seemed familiar, too."

"And then there's …"

"What?"

He gaze drifted away again. "Sometimes …"

"What, Mike?"

"Sometimes it seems like I hear a voice in my head. It's very low, and he's speaking some kind of Latin dialect I can't quite make out."

"Michael!" I gasped. "Don't you know who that is?"

His eyes came up to mine. "Well, I'm thinking it's my own subconscious trying to accommodate all this weirdness."

"Mike, they're trying to tell us something. Both of them. Can't you see that?"

He shook his head. "I don't like this, Anne. I mean, I like you. In fact, I'm almost insanely attracted to you, but …"

"But, all this paranormal stuff is really freaking you out," I finished for him.

"Yeah," he admitted, "it is."

I smiled. "Not to mention the fact that I'm a nun."

"That too."

"Well," I said, "I'm leaving the day after tomorrow. Then your life can get back to normal."

"I don't know. It feels like nothing'll ever be normal again."

I couldn't think what to say, so I just sat and watched him.

His dark eyes were alive in the candlelight. "And," he went on, "crazy as it sounds, I don't want you to go. I want you to stay with me. I feel like …"

"Like we belong together?"

"Yes."

I just sat there, looking back at him.

"Can you relate to that?"

I laid my glass down. "Part of me can," I said. "But I don't know which part."

His gaze was intense.

I tried again. "What I mean is, I don't know if it would be Anne or …"

"Or Daphne," he finished.

"Right."

"Well," he said, standing up, "let me know when you get that one sorted out. I only want to be with one woman at a time." He dropped a few euros on the table, and we headed for the door.

We walked back to the apartment in silence, not touching. Above us the trees swayed in the evening breeze. In the distance the mountain grumbled, and the sidewalk trembled slightly under our feet.

When we got back to his place, he asked me with what seemed excessive politeness if I wanted the bathroom first. "No, you go ahead," I told him, and he disappeared behind the closed door. I heard the water running in the sink. Something about that felt oddly intimate.

When he came out, he glanced over and gave me a nod and a vague smile. "Night" was all he said.

"Goodnight," I said. "Thanks for dinner."

He crossed quickly to the old desk in the corner, picked up his laptop, and carried it over to the bed. I watched him turn on his small bedside lamp and climb in fully clothed in tee shirt and shorts. Propped up on the pillows, he started recording his day's notes.

I turned over, burrowed under my blanket, and lay there for some time wishing we weren't on such strained terms. I toyed with the idea of getting up and going over there to speak to him. But I didn't know what to say any more than he did, and anyway, I had no business on that side of the room. Finally his light went off. I lay back on the pillow and closed my eyes. Voicelessly, so as not to disturb him, I began my Hail Marys.

I'm not sure when sleep finally came.

Chapter 15

F resh from the baths, oiled and perfumed, I am hurrying about my errands. It is late in the day now, and I need to get home to prepare an evening meal for my husband and son. I stop at a wine shop and buy a small jug of sweet red, then at the poultry monger's for a freshly roasted chicken and some boiled eggs. With the last of my denarii, I go into Paulus's bakery and ask for a fresh-baked loaf and a small pot of honey.

Alexander is already there when I get upstairs. He comes to me at once and takes my laden basket, examining the contents as he carries it to the eating corner. I see him pull out the honey and beam with childish pleasure.

"Alexander," I say, "I will need some water. Go down to the fountain for me, will you?"

His smile widens, and he picks up the bucket by the door.

"Oh, and Alexander?"

He stops, turns to me.

"Take the cloth and clean yourself while you are down there. You have dust all over your arms and legs."

He nods, still grinning. "I will, Mother. I'll be back soon."

I watch him slip through the door and close it with a bang. I hear his footsteps tripping lightly down the steps. But my eyes stay riveted on the doorway. Just for an instant, another boy is there—a smaller boy with blond curls, smiling, holding a large ball. My unreasoned impulse is to reach out. *Stop! Don't go!* Then the little boy is gone, and I am left with a vague, gnawing anxiety in my chest. *Don't go.*

Compulsively, I go to the balcony and watch Alexander emerge from under it. He motions to the dog, which pelts after him as he runs up the street, the bucket bouncing along at his side. He is just going to the fountain, I tell myself, but a shadowy sense of foreboding makes me want to call him back, to hold him. The boards beneath my feet tremble as I stand there, and a deep, rumbling comes from the mountain. Have faith, I assure myself, the goddess will take care of us. Still, I wish fervently that my husband would come home.

⊕ ⊕ ⊕

Mike's alarm went off, and I heard him groan and shut it off. Then I heard the bed springs creak as he got up. A moment later, he appeared at the open balcony doors.

"Morning," he said.

I found myself standing there at the railing, staring into nothingness.

"Anne?"

Reality snapped back into place. I turned to face him. "Morning," I said with a fake smile.

"What are you doing?"

"I have no idea," I told him honestly.

He leaned on the doorjamb in tee-shirt and boxers and regarded me gravely. "Another dream?" he asked.

I nodded.

"You okay?"

"Yes," I assured him. "I woke up, and I came out here for some air."

He frowned, and his eyes scrutinized me for a moment. Finally, he nodded. "Okay, I'm going to go take a shower."

"Fine," I said. "You go ahead. I'm all right, really."

He gave me one more wary look then turned and headed for the bathroom. I heard him flushing, running the water, brushing his teeth. Eventually he came out in his usual cutoffs and a clean, sleeveless shirt. I was melting butter in a pan to fry some eggs.

I felt his approach but didn't look up.

"Anne …" He was leaning on the serving counter. I could feel his eyes on me.

"Yes?'

"I don't want you to leave, but I'm afraid that this place really isn't very good for you."

I stopped with the spatula in my hand. The steel bands around my rib cage began to tighten, and I suddenly felt sick. "You're kicking me out?" I said without looking up.

"No, Anne, it's not that."

I turned to him. "What is it then?"

He blew out a heavy sigh. "Look, I'm due for a break, and I haven't been back to the States for months. I could go with you. We could get you checked out. You know, make sure you're all right."

I cracked an egg into the pan. "I don't want to leave Herculaneum," I said flatly. "At least not right now. Tomorrow is …"

"Yes," he said, "tomorrow is the twenty-fourth."

I met his eyes directly. "I have to be here, Mike. After tomorrow night I'll go, okay?"

He ran a hand through his damp hair. "Okay, we don't have to figure this out right now. But maybe we could talk about it tonight."

"Okay," I said, stirring the scrambled eggs.

I loaded our plates and carried them to the table. We ate in silence for several minutes. Finally I got up the nerve to speak.

"So," I said, pushing my eggs with my fork, "can I still go with you this afternoon?"

He looked at me. "You really think you're up to it?"

I looked back. "Up to it? Of course, I am. I feel great."

"I can't watch you every minute, you know. I have work to do."

"I'll be fine."

After a while he said, "This is it, Anne. After today, you need to stay out of Herculaneum. It's doing something to your mind, and I don't think it's anything good."

"Are we back to that?" I asked him. "You think I'm crazy?"

"No, you're not crazy. I just think all this is making you ill. It's keeping you awake; you're having nightmares when you do sleep; you're walking around confused. Hell, you don't even know where you are half the time."

I put out my hand and touched his. "Mike, you're right. I'm a mess, and it can't go on. I know that. But, this is something I've just got to do. Daphne's trying to tell me something. She's reaching out to me."

"Anne, do you hear yourself?"

"Can't you see how strong she is?"

His eyes blazed back at me. "Then you have to be stronger. She can't just escape her life by invading yours. You've got to fight this!"

"I'm trying, Mike!"

"Not hard enough!"

I snatched my hand away. "Why have you turned against me? Last night I thought you understood."

"Well, I don't," he said, dropping his fork. "I don't understand any of this." He stopped, took a deep breath, gazed out the window. "But I'm …" His eyes flicked up to mine for a moment then dropped. "I'm here, you know that."

"Will you wait?" I pressed. "Will you let me see this through?"

He finally met my gaze directly, and his warm brown eyes were full of tumbling emotion for a moment. Then he shrugged. "Do I have a choice?"

"Of course you do," I said. "But I'm asking. Will you?"

"What am I supposed to do, restrain you bodily? Call the local police? Put a twenty-four hour watch on you?"

I shook my head. "You won't do that."

After a moment he said, "No."

"Thank you, Marc."

His eyes narrowed, and his brow creased into a frown.

"What?" I said. "What is it?"

"You looked … I don't know … different just then."

"Different?"

"Yeah, your expression. And your eyes, they looked … I don't know … darker somehow. And that voice …"

I stared at him. "You saw her," I said breathlessly. "You saw Daphne."

He got up. "No, I saw you. And for a minute you looked different. Now, that's all the supernatural bullshit I can handle for one morning."

"Okay," I said.

"Excuse the language."

"It's all right."

He took his plate to the kitchen. "Look," he said busily, "I'll be back here around noon, and if you're ready, I'll get you back into Herculaneum one more time, but that's it, okay?"

"Okay." I stood at the end of the kitchen counter watching him.

He was rinsing his plate at the sink. "Look, Anne …" he began tentatively.

"No, no." I held up a hand. "It's all right. I understand why you'd be uncomfortable with all this. Me and my dreams and all the weirdness. It's okay. It's almost over."

He paused, holding his plate, not looking at me. "I didn't say I wanted it to be over." Then he added slowly, quietly, "Not for us, I mean."

"Mike …"

Now his eyes came up to meet mine. "I just want you to be all right. I'm afraid for you."

"I know."

He dropped his dish towel and came over to me. His eyes locked on mine. "Don't you know how it is with me?"

I felt my heart racing, the beginnings of panic. He was too real, too physical, too close! "Mike," I told him, "I'm not ready."

His gaze was steady now. "I know. But there it is anyway."

It would have been so easy to fall into those dark eyes. No eyes had looked at me that way for so long. Marcus looks at her that way, with that longing, that desire.

"I wish …" I began and then couldn't continue.

He took another step closer, took my face in his two hands, and kissed my lips gently. I closed my eyes and felt his fingers in my hair, the warmth, the soft pressure of his lips. His scent was strong, heady. My hands came up to touch his rib cage. I could feel his heartbeat.

Then his lips pulled away. He laid his forehead against mine and stood there for a few seconds, eyes closed, forearms resting on my shoulders. I saw his erection and felt compassion. How strange, not to be able to hide your feelings in that way.

Abruptly he straightened and turned away. "Okay," he said, grabbing his backpack, "I'm going now." He stepped around me, where I stood frozen, and made for the door. On the threshold he stopped and stood for a moment, holding it open. "You sure you're going to be okay here?"

I nodded. "Yes, Mike, don't worry."

He nodded. "I'll see you at noon." And he was gone.

I stood there and had a conversation with myself:

Do you want this man, or don't you? I don't know. *You can't just keep stringing him along like this.* I know. *Do you really want to be loved again?* I don't know. *Can you handle that?* No. I don't know. No, not yet.

Sleep, I told myself, that's all I really want. I turned and made my way across the room, passing the sofa and moving instead over to the bed, Mike's bed. I pulled off my dress and then my bra and panties. It was her life I wanted as I crawled naked under the covers. I wanted Alexander, Marcus …

Interlude IX

I am losing patience with her, Marcus.

    So soon?

She is in the prime of life. She has beauty, a quick mind, good health—everything the gods can bestow on a woman. She has a whole lifetime of experience stretching out before her. And now this good man wants to love her, yet she shrinks away. All those gifts are wasted on her.

    The woman is wounded, Daphne. She has known great misfortune.

Yes, but must she be crippled by it? I would like to shake her.

    Why does this trouble you so?

Because I did not have my life! There was no time. And here she is, turning away from all that I wanted and had taken from me.

    Daphne, when you had your chance for happiness, you pushed it away, too.

You say this to me now, Marcus? After all this time?

I only say it to remind you how hard the picture is to see when you are living it. I too have regrets.

I see.

But you do not speak?

I am pondering the wisdom of your words.

Come, Daphne, do not be bitter. You spoke of compassion. That is what this woman needs.

Anne.

Anne, yes. But you miss my point.

No, there is truth in what you say. But compassion is not always gentle. I would show her what real death is. Then perhaps she will not long for it, as though it were somehow nobler than life.

Chapter 16

I expected Marcus home hours ago. Now the lamps are lit, and Alexander and I are eating our supper alone. I watch in silence as he dips his bread into the bowl of honey. He finishes his last bite and reclines on one elbow, chewing, relishing the sweetness. His gleaming eyes smile across the table at me. "Do not worry, Mother," he finally says, "Father will be home soon. It will be well between you."

I flush slightly, embarrassed that my young son should feel it necessary to give me such advice. "Thank you, Alexander," I say a bit stiffly. "Perhaps you should go to your bed now so that I can talk with him when he does come."

His young face squeezes into an uncharacteristic frown. "But I want to see him too!"

"I know, loved one, but mothers and fathers need some time alone to …" I search for the words. "To be happy together." He gazes back at me tentatively. "Do you understand what I am saying to you?"

Alexander considers this for a moment, then nods solemnly. "I think so," he says. "And I do want you and Father to be happy. I want us to be a real family." He gets up and stretches his arms in an exaggerated yawn. "I believe I am getting tired," he says with a conspiratorial smile.

I catch his small hand in mine. "You are my little man," I tell him. "You are growing up before my eyes."

His fingers brush my temple. "Soon you will have two men to look after you."

"Yes," I say. "Fortuna is kind."

Alexander turns and crosses the room to the draped doorway that leads to his little cubicle. He pauses there to turn and angle me another smile. "I will study my numerals for my lesson tomorrow." I stop him before he can pull back the drape.

"Alexander?"

"Yes?"

"I am sorry about the festival."

"There will be lots of festivals." He gives me one last smile then steps into his alcove and draws the curtain.

Aphrodite, I pray silently as I clear away the dinner things, lend me your gifts. Make me beautiful in my husband's eyes. Let it be as it was before between us. Oh, I want so much to be happy again.

I go to my dressing table and sit on the bench. Taking up the polished bronze hand mirror my former mistress gave me, I examine my face. It is not the smooth, young girl's face Marcus left eight years ago. There are lines around the eyes from squinting at my work, and small creases at the corners of my mouth. It is not an old face, not unattractive, I just haven't taken care of it like the rich ladies do. Now I wish I had. How much trouble would it have been, after all, to smooth on a bit of olive oil at night?

Still, I can at least put on a little makeup, fix my hair the way he used to like it. I open a small jar of berry-tinted ointment for my lips and begin smoothing it on with my fingertip. My hair is still long and dark and luxuriant. Tomorrow maybe I will buy some wine and soak it to bring out the reddish highlights. I reach for a second jar of dark paste and a small brush. The ladies at the temple of Isis all line their eyes this way to make them look large and beautiful.

The door latch rattles, then the hinges creak as the old door swings slowly open.

My prayer is answered! Marcus is standing there holding a large, flat, oblong package. His face breaks into a broad smile.

"Husband!" I cry as I rush forward. He has been to the baths. He is clean shaven, and his skin is warm and scented with oils as I embrace him. "I was worried," I breathe against his neck. "You were gone so long!"

"I am sorry. I had an important errand."

"All is well, my love," I tell him as I unpin his cloak. "You are home now."

His eyes scan the room. "Where is the boy?"

I nod toward Alexander's cubicle.

Marcus sets down his package and steps quietly over to open the drape a bit. He stands there for several heartbeats, looking down at the sleeping child. Then he turns back to me, his eyes glistening.

I press two fingers to my lips in a gesture that says, let him sleep.

He nods and closes the curtain. For a moment we stand gazing at each other. Then he turns to retrieve the mysterious package he has left by the door. Carefully he picks it up and holds it out to me. It is padded and wrapped in several layers of cloth. "Open it," he says.

"For me?" My voice sounds almost girlish.

He nods. "I brought it from Jerusalem."

I take the package and carry it over to the sitting couch. Carefully I undo the wrappings. When the last of the padding is removed, something shiny catches the lamplight.

"Here," Marcus says, coming forward to take the object out for me. He holds it up, smiling.

It is magnificent! A polished silver mirror big enough to see my entire head and upper body. The looking plate is as smooth and flawless as still water, and around the edges some master craftsman has hammered and pressed out an intricate pattern that resembles a complicated rope. Its rounded, serpentine edges send tiny shafts of light splaying out across the room. "Oh, Marcus!" I whisper. "It must have been so expensive!"

He nods. "We found it in a big empty house, the home of some rich Jewish family before Emperor Titus drove them all out of the city nine years ago. They had left a lot of personal belongings behind."

"How sad," I muse, drawing my fingertip slowly across the shining surface, "to be driven out of one's home."

Marcus stands up straighter, a military posture. "Yes, it was a hard thing, but you cannot blame the emperor. The place was out of control. Constant rioting and uprisings. The emperor gave the rebels a chance to surrender the city, but they refused. He had no choice."

I nod at this explanation and put a smile back on my face.

"Anyway," Marcus goes on, "the house was to be razed, so I claimed this for you." He sets the mirror upright on my dressing table then turns back to me. "So you can see how beautiful you are to me."

I come slowly forward and sit on my bench. The image is so clear it is like seeing myself for the first time. My eyes look bright, my skin pink. I gaze up at Marcus's reflection as he stands behind me, still smiling. He places his hand gently on my shoulder, and I bend my neck to kiss it. Then I take my fingertip and run it over the mirror's many surfaces, wondering at its shining perfection. Some great lady owned this, and now it is here on my dressing table.

"It is wonderful, Marcus," I breathe, "but it is much too fine for me."

"Nothing is too fine for you. To me you are an empress, a goddess."

I lean my head back on his stomach. "Oh, Marcus, I have missed you so much!"

Slowly, quietly, he starts pulling the tangled locks, one by one, from the thick twist on the back of my head. I watch in the mirror as the tresses come down, tumbling thick and dark around my face and shoulders. When it is loose, he reaches for my ivory comb and begins to draw it gently through the tangles. Then he pulls the gleaming mass of hair to one side and tenderly combs the tendrils on my neck with his fingers.

And it happens. Eight years of separation melt away. I feel the quietness, then the physical sensation of warmth rising up from somewhere in my midsection, and then the euphoria, the outward flowing of tension. I shiver as the feeling reaches my neck, and then it is in my head, in my mind. I sigh and am at peace. More than at peace, I am floating in gentleness, in love.

I look up at him and smile, softly, almost shyly.

His dark eyes gaze back at me, full of desire.

I rise and turn to face him. His arms close around my waist.

Interlude X

I think it must have been her son I saw. A small boy, younger than Alexander, golden haired. Once he was holding a large ball.

Where was this?

In my … our home. And even before that, when I was watching Alexander run up the street. His hair turned to gold.

That proves nothing. You could have imagined …

No, I saw her too, Marcus, and not just in dreams. She was in the temple. I even heard her voice.

The temple?

Aphrodite's temple.

You never mentioned this before.

I did not understand. I was afraid of her. When I first started dreaming, I thought she might be a daemon. Then in the temple I took her for a foreigner. And, later I actually thought she was Aphrodite.

Aphrodite! You thought she was the goddess?

She was beautiful, Marcus. Very tall and dressed all in white, and her hair was golden like the statues. I had been praying, and then suddenly, there she was. She spoke to me in a strange tongue. I tried to offer her Alexander's talisman to appease her.

That was a Christian pendant!

It was all I had.

And did she accept this offering?

No, she screamed at me.

Chapter 17

It must have been a tremor that awakened me, or maybe a distant roll of thunder. The morning had darkened, and through the balcony doors I could see the trees swaying, casting moving gray shadows across the glass. I closed my eyes and lay back, trying to hold on to the dream, trying to call it back. Marcus was there. My Marcus.

But it was no good, the vision was gone. I was alone, in Mike DeMarco's bed.

I gathered the pillow in my arms and held it against my bare skin. I didn't want to be alone in this place. I wanted Marcus. Alexander, Barry, Sean, Mike ... someone. *Oh, stop this! Stop it!*

I took a deep breath and turned to a favorite old Psalm for comfort. "The Lord is my shepherd. I shall not want. He maketh me to lie down ..."

Another tremor interrupted my concentration. It was so slight that if it had not been for my supine stillness, I might not even have noticed it. But it was there, a subtle rolling of the floorboards, and a rumbling sound, deep and ominous. I turned my head to the balcony doors, where a weak light was filtering through. There was no hope of getting back to sleep.

I got up, threw on Mike's oversized shirt, and swung open the balcony doors. The wind caught my hair and whipped it into my eyes as I stood barefoot at the railing. When I lowered my head, I noticed a small crack in the concrete deck that hadn't been there before. Slight or no, the tremors were real. And the distant rumblings of the mountain. Just like before the eruption.

Oh, Daphne, I thought suddenly, *get out. Get out now!*

She needed me. I was sure of it. She had called me here to help her. But what could I do? How could I save them? Their bones were lying down there in the sand. It had all happened two thousand years ago, and I wasn't *there*, Daphne! *I wasn't there, and I couldn't do anything!*

I got a quick flash of my son, poised in the doorway, smiling. His father standing just behind him, his hand on the boy's shoulder. *"We'll be back this afternoon, Mother."*

No, my mind screamed, *don't go! Don't go!*

I shook my head to clear the vision. Was it Alexander and Marcus I'd seen, or was it Sean and Barry? It was all blurring together somehow. I was losing control.

I went back inside and lay down on the bed. If I could just dream. If I could go back there and warn them somehow …

But sleep didn't come. I just lay on my back and listened to the raindrops pelt down briefly and then subside. I was still lying there with my eyes closed when I heard a knock on the door. I stirred myself and went to answer it, running fingers through my tangled hair as I went.

"Who is it?" I called.

"It's Jan Goodman," came a voice from the other side.

I opened the door quickly. There she stood in her safari shorts and a slightly damp tee, sizing up my disheveled appearance with sharp black eyes.

I stepped back. "Come in, Dr. Goodman."

"Call me Jan," she said brusquely as she strode past. I closed the door then turned to find her standing in the middle of the room, hands in her pockets, shoulders stiff, thin body poised to spring. Everything about her bristled negative energy.

"Mike's not here," I told her.

"I know," she clipped. "I came to see you."

"Oh," I said in consternation. "Well, would you like to sit down?" As I said it, I heard myself playing hostess.

She stalked over to a dining chair and sat at the table.

"Coffee?" I said.

She shot me a quick, dark glance. "Yeah, I'll have a cup, if it's made."

I went into the kitchen. "Cream or sugar?"

"Black."

I poured each of us a mug and carried them to the table. Sat down. Waited.

She took a tentative sip, eyeing me from over the rim. There was a coiled hostility in those eyes, a faint rattle in her stillness.

Finally I couldn't take it anymore. "So, Dr. Goodman … Jan, what brings you here?"

"It's about Mike," she began.

I didn't like the sound of it, but I prompted her anyway. "Yes? What about Mike?"

Her nostrils flared slightly as she fingered the handle of her cup. "You two seem to be getting quite close."

I sipped and swallowed. "Close friends, yes."

"Is that all it is to you?"

I looked across at her, amused. "Are you asking me about my intentions?"

She set her mug down. "He thinks he's in love with you."

I shook my head and smiled into my coffee. "No, I'm sure you're mistaken. We've only known each other for a few days."

"But you're living here," she said flatly.

"It's only temporary. I'm leaving the day after tomorrow."

Her eyes bore into mine. "So I hear, and Mike thinks he's going with you."

"Well," I hedged, "he did mention something like that, but …"

"Look," she said, leaning forward in her chair, "I'm Mike's major professor. I pulled strings to get him on this project, and he needs the research for his dissertation. This is no time for him to jump up and go chasing off after you."

"Wait a minute," I said indignantly, "I never asked Mike to do anything of the kind. If he's come up with some idea to go back to the States for a little while, that's his business. He's an adult."

Her next words came out with bitten precision. "He's one of the brightest graduate students I've ever had. He'll be a PhD at twenty-six and a prime candidate for a tenure-track professorship. He's got too much to lose to be sidetracked right now. You need to back away."

I sat back and felt my hackles rising. "If you don't mind the observation, Dr. Goodman, you seem to have quite a proprietary interest in this student. Maybe it's you who should back away."

Her eyes narrowed to dark slits. "Don't try that offended lady crap on me. You're not a kid. You know exactly what you're doing."

"And just what do you think I'm doing?"

"You're seducing a young man who tried to help you, and you don't care that you're endangering his future."

I sat there, astonished. Me, a seductress? Me, Anne McCarthy, who'd only had one lover in her life? Who instinctively shied away from anyone who tried to get close? Who'd systematically shut off all emotion and drawn myself into a ball? Suddenly I was luring young men to their ruin? It was so surreal that I actually gave a short laugh.

Jan Goodman jumped to her feet and glared down at me. "Listen," she hissed, "you may think this is funny, but you're fucking with a man's life here! I don't know what your game is, but if you have any decency, you'll get back on that tour bus and go back where you came from before you do any more damage!"

I rose with dignity. "Thank you for coming, Dr. Goodman, but your concern is misplaced." I started for the door. "I can see that you have a personal investment in Michael, but you don't need to worry. I am here conducting my own research, and it will be finished by tomorrow. I'll be going back to America the following day, and I plan on going alone."

She stood in the doorway as I held it open. Her jet eyes were hard and glittering. "Glad to hear it," she snapped, then she turned and strode off down the hallway in her thick-soled hiking shoes.

I closed the door and leaned against it for a few moments, feeling strangely titillated. What an odd encounter! No one had ever accused me of being a temptress before. Not me. Daphne, maybe.

I straightened suddenly. *Daphne!* She was a beautiful woman, sensuous, seductive. Was I actually turning into Daphne? Was I losing myself entirely to her? The next thought came suddenly, before I could censor it. *Do I want to?*

I wandered over and folded my blanket and arranged it and my pillow on the couch. Next I went over and made Mike's bed. Then I stood up and looked around me. This place needs work, I thought coolly. I started at once, busying myself around the apartment, cleaning, tidying, organizing his books. I swept the floors and the old, threadbare rug, rearranged and wiped down the kitchen counters. Then I noticed the time and began making lunch—fried green peppers with melted cheese and tomato sauce over pasta. I was showered, fully dressed, and had the table set when Mike got home.

When he came through the door, he paused, and his eyes swept the room slowly. Then he turned to where I was standing near the table and gave me a penetrating look.

I gave him back only friendliness, cheerfulness, lightness. Pulling off the towel I'd been using for an apron, I gestured toward the waiting plates. "Well," I said in a voice that sounded too high, "come and sit down. Lunch is all ready."

He closed the door and stepped forward, his eyes fixed on me. I smiled and pulled back his chair.

Mike seated himself quietly, as if everything might crack and disappear if he moved too quickly. I sat across from him. "Well," I said brightly, "try it. It's my own concoction."

"Thanks," he finally said, "this is great."

I rolled a forkful of pasta and put it in my mouth. It tasted good, but for some reason, it was hard to swallow. I smiled across at him.

He took a bite. "It's terrific. Really."

I smiled, chewing.

"I can't believe you did all this."

I shrugged. "It's the least I can do."

"I hope you didn't think you had to pay me back or something."

"No, not at all," I assured him. "I just needed something useful to do."

He nodded and went back to his food. I waited until he had a mouthful of spaghetti before I said, "Dr. Goodman was here."

He looked up and swallowed. "Here? In the apartment?"

I pointed. "That exact spot, in fact."

"What'd she want?"

"She wanted to talk to me." I took a sip of ice water. "About you."

He squinched up his face. "What?"

"She thinks I'm distracting you from your work. She wants me to go home before I do any more damage."

"What is she, my mother?"

"I'm afraid I was a little curt to her. I don't know what came over me. She was just so aggressive, it put my back up. I hope I didn't cause any trouble for you."

He waved this off. "Don't worry about it. I've always thought she was a little *too* concerned about me. Sometimes I feel like she's looking up my shorts."

For some reason, I found that picture ridiculously funny, and I had to stifle a giggle. Mike went back to his stuffed peppers while I regained my composure.

I took another sip of water and said, "So how's the dig going? Anything new?"

He nodded. "We found some more skeletons this morning." I expected him to go on, but he stopped.

"Yes?" I prompted.

He looked down and addressed his pasta. "One's a woman," he said.

I set my fork down and stared at him.

"She was between twenty-five and thirty. Jan says she was a beautiful woman, judging from her bone structure." He took another bite and did not look up.

"Where?" I almost whispered.

He sipped from his water glass. "On the beach, forty yards or so from where we found the soldier."

"Mike …" I said.

Now he looked up. "I know what you're thinking, but it could be anyone. It's not necessarily her."

"It's her," I said.

"Anne, you're not going down there."

"Okay," I said calmly.

"I mean it."

"Okay."

He blotted his lips with a napkin. "I want your word, or I'm not taking you into Herculaneum today."

"Okay, you have it." But something cold and hard and determined was forming in my chest as I looked back at him.

I spent the long, steamy afternoon wandering among the ruins. Three times I walked past the old staircase and continued down the block, resisting its draw on me. The fourth time I stopped and regarded the grillwork and the rickety steps for a few moments. Then I stepped forward and grasped the bars in my hands. I stood there gazing up, knowing what was up there. Her loom, her couches, her dressing table. It was probably seared and blackened, but it was all still there. I knew it. I closed my eyes and pressed my forehead against the iron bars. The dizziness came suddenly.

"Alexander," I say urgently, "where did you get this?"

I am holding a small object in my hand, a talisman. The metal is dark and heavy, but the shape it forms is done in delicate filigree so that it has a substantial but not weighty feel in my hand. It hangs from a finely wrought copper chain around my son's neck. The talisman is in the shape of a fish.

Alexander looks up at me with dark, puzzled eyes. "Father gave it to me. He said to carry it in my neck pouch, that it would bring me good luck and protect me from bad spirits." He smiles. "Father has one too, but his is gold, and the fish has painted colors on its scales."

"Alexander, you must not wear that in the city. You don't know what it means. It is a symbol for a radical Eastern religious cult. It is dangerous to be seen wearing one of these!"

"But why?" he asks, wide-eyed.

"Because if the Praetorian Guards see it, they will arrest you! They will come and arrest us all! Give it to me. I will get rid of it. Alexander!"

I stepped back from the bars and stumbled out onto the old cobbles. This vision had unsettled me like no other, and I was trembling. Something about the talisman, something terrible. Some grief not yet realized but pending.

I turned and paced off quickly, up the ancient street. At the corner I turned right, toward the temple. I was on the Decumanus Maximus now, walking faster, more purposefully. I had a destination. I knew exactly where I was going.

Until I came to an abrupt halt at the edge of the excavation. Where the forum should have been, there was a sheer mud wall. The street went nowhere. I turned slowly. A jumble of incomprehensible images came suddenly, with a jolt.

I am standing at the top of a stone staircase, looking out into darkness. Piercing the gloom, swift-moving balls of flame chase across my field of vision like ghosts on the wind. There is something ghastly about the sight, as if some giant maw waits to swallow them. Beneath the roaring sound, I hear occasional shouts, screams, a child crying. These are souls, I realize, being pulled to their extinction by some unseen force. I am standing at the gates of Hades ...

The vision cleared as quickly as it had come, and I found myself staring at the ragged grass and empty pool of the praetorium. The old athletic field spread before me in placid silence. A solitary bird perched stolidly on the top of one of the cracked columns.

I walked away in a daze, bewildered, back the way I'd come. And inevitably my feet found their way back to the staircase. I stood there, pressing my forehead to the iron bars, eyes closed, breathing hard.

Alexander you must not wear that in the city. It is dangerous ... dangerous ... dangerous ...!

The voice lingered in my head, and the feel of the fish-shaped talisman in my hand. I knew it for what it was, a sacred symbol of Early Christianity, so why did it disturb me so? Even as I stood there, I felt the panic in my chest. What about it? What about the talisman?

But the moment passed, and the visions faded. I pushed away from the bars and turned back down Cardo V, this time with no destination in mind, only a vague feeling that I had lost something, that I was searching for something. Crossing the Decumanus Inferior, I pushed on toward the harbor.

It wasn't until I saw a male figure down at the end standing at the terrace railing, his outline dark against the glow of the western sky, that I knew my destination. With a gasp of relief, I rushed forward. As I got closer his dark hair and beard took shape. My lips formed the word "Marcus," and I started running. He was just a few yards away before I realized who it was.

I came to a halt in front of him. "I've been looking for you."

Mike stood there, dusty, bristle-faced, hair ruffling in the evening breeze. The pull of his eyes was strong. "I've been looking for you, too" was all he said.

We stood there staring at each other for several moments, then I took the hand he was holding out to me and followed him down the terrace to the ramp.

Chapter 18

We found a small sidewalk bistro on one of Ercolano's back streets, and Mike ordered for us in Italian. Oddly, we didn't talk while we waited for the wine. He simply laid his hand on the table, palm up, and I took it. His fingers closed gently around mine, and we just sat there letting our pulses synchronize. A minute or two flowed by before the waiter appeared, plunked a carafe of red wine and two glasses down on our table, muttered something in Italian, and left. Mike let go of my hand and poured us each a glass. Then he lifted his toward me.

I brought mine up, too. "What are we toasting?"

"Just us. Just being here. It might be our last night."

I stared at him.

"Your last night here, I mean."

"Oh," I said and clinked the rim of my glass to his. I took a sip then held my glass to the candle glowing on our table, watching the clear red liquid tremble. "Mike ..." I began.

"Don't," he said softly.

I tried again, calmly and carefully. "I just wanted to thank you ..."

"Don't say it. Just be here with me tonight."

I gave him a bittersweet smile.

He reached up and took a curling lock of my hair in his fingers. "It's so beautiful in the candlelight."

"I almost cut it on the ship," I volunteered.

"Why?"

"Because … I don't know." I shrugged. "I guess it just seemed too showy. Too sensuous maybe."

He smiled. "There's no such thing as too sensuous."

I looked down and sipped my wine.

"Anne, why do you fight it so hard? Being a woman."

I answered obliquely. "On my twelfth birthday, my mother invited the whole family over for a party. All day she fussed over my hair. Vinegar rinse, special shampoo and conditioner, curling iron. For a finishing touch she gathered up the top part and fixed it in a ponytail with little fake blue flowers to match my dress. The rest of it fell down my back in ringlets. I looked like Shirley Temple. But her face in the mirror was so happy and proud as she stood behind me admiring her work.

"When I made my appearance downstairs, everybody kept looking at it and touching it and saying how pretty it was. They hardly looked at me at all. It was just about my precious hair. And worst of all, my cousin Billy kept sneaking up behind me and pulling on it. He'd yank on a ringlet then dance away laughing, leering at me.

"After they all left, I crept upstairs to my mother's dressing table, took her scissors, and started cutting it off, lock by lock. I was about halfway through when my mom came in. I looked up from the mirror and saw her standing there in the doorway. Her eyes dropped to the pile of curls on the floor, and when they came back up to me …" I stopped to swallow hard. "They were full of tears."

"Why'd you do it?" Mike asked.

I shook my head to fight back my own tears. "I felt foolish, like some stupid little doll that everybody wanted to touch and play with."

He withdrew instantly. "I'm sorry. The last thing I wanted was to upset you."

I was looking at my wine glass. When I spoke it was a non sequitur. "I didn't mind when Barry touched my hair." Then I looked up into his candlelit eyes, gazing back at me so earnestly. "I don't mind when you do." I took his hand again. I brought it up slowly and placed it on the side of my head.

"Don't ever cut your hair off," he said, stroking my cheek with his fingertips. "It's part of you. But it's not all of you. When I first saw you I thought you had beautiful bone structure. And you had mysterious, smoky green eyes that kept sliding away."

I smiled a little.

"But since you've been here, you've taken on a new kind of beauty. Your face has lost that tight, gaunt look. Your skin glows. Your eyes are lit from within. It's you, not your hair."

My eyes narrowed slightly. "Is it me, or is it ... her?"

His fingers held my chin firmly as he leaned forward. "It's you, Anne. She's not here, she's dead. But you're alive. You're here and warm and alive right now, and love is staring you in the face. Stop hiding from it. Have courage and live!"

I don't know how I would have answered. I was sitting there with welling eyes studying his face, so close to mine. So close ....

"Scusa!" said the waiter, and he plopped a plate of linguine down in front of me. Mike dropped his hand, and I sat back quickly, embarrassed, almost relieved.

No one spoke while I poked at the food on my plate.

"Anne ..."

I shook my head slightly and didn't look up.

The silence elongated, charging the air.

"Anne ...," he repeated.

I began rolling a few strands of pasta against my plate. "So," I said breezily, "tell me about your dissertation timetable."

He stared back at me. I watched a series of fleeting emotions drift across his features. Then his eyes fell, and he dove into his own food.

The rest of the dinner was a blur. Small talk: the food, the weather forecast, his career prospects, my plans for the return trip. The subtext was too sensitive to touch, and we left it alone.

He just took my hand as we walked home and said nothing more until we got there. We climbed the stairs in silence. I felt his breath in my hair as he reached around me on the landing to open the door.

I took a few steps into the room then turned when I heard it click shut. He stood there in the semidarkness, just inside the door, watching me. "You want to sit on the balcony for a while?" he asked me.

"Actually I'm pretty tired," I said.

He nodded. "Me too. Guess I'll turn in, then."

He disappeared into the bathroom. I could hear his electric toothbrush humming as I made up my bed on the couch. I was cool. I was detached. He was a stranger in there brushing his teeth. It had nothing to do with me.

He came out wearing only boxer shorts and headed directly for the bed. I watched surreptitiously as he strode across the room. His body was lean, less muscled than Marcus's, but there was a sleekness to it and a certain quick grace. I watched him stop at the bed, hesitate, then turn back to me. There was something brave and poignant about the way he stood there. Even in the dim light, I could feel him asking me a question with his eyes.

"Goodnight, Mike," I said.

"Night," he said softly, and I heard the bed springs as he climbed in and tossed in the covers for a minute or so. Then he fell quiet, and I lay down on the couch fully clothed and pulled the blanket around me. After a moment I threw it off. It was hotter than usual tonight, and I couldn't get comfortable.

For what might have been an hour, I lay there waiting for sleep. Mike was snoring softly, and somehow that soothed, rather than annoyed me. I finally admitted to myself that I didn't want to lie here on this sofa alone, not tonight. Quietly I took my pillow, got up, and padded over to the bed, placing my bare feet carefully on the old boards so they wouldn't creak. Cautiously I lifted the edge of the sheet and eased myself under the covers. I stayed on my own side. I lay quietly so as not to wake him. I listened to his breathing and felt … safe.

⊕　⊕　⊕

"I'm sorry, Daphne," Marcus whispers against my neck. "I'm sorry you were alone all these years. I didn't write as often as I should have, but all I dreamed about was you, coming home to you and the boy."

"Oh, it doesn't matter," I say fervently. "It doesn't matter, Marcus. You're here with me now. Don't ever leave me again!"

His lips are on mine then. His face is smooth, and his breath smells of cloves, and he is tall and strong, and he is my husband. I clutch greedily at him like a starving woman.

"Ah, Daphne, I've travelled all over the world, but you are the most beautiful woman …"

"Shhhh, let's not wake Alexander. Come. Make love to me."

He is lifting me off my feet, carrying me through the draped opening to my inner chamber, laying me carefully on the narrow mattress. There is no lamp, but in the dark I feel him, hear his breathing, smell the sweetness of his clean, manly scent.

I lie passively, expectantly, while he sits on the edge of the bed and slowly removes my shift. He sits for a moment, gazing at my body, then his hand comes up to touch me. My breath comes in short gasps as he caresses my skin. I feel my heart thudding inside my chest.

I lie there, still and naked in the darkness, and watch his dim outline as he bends to pull off his sandals. Then he stands. Slowly, taking his time, he unbuckles his belt and his leather breast plate. They fall to the floor, one soft thud and then another. He slips his tunic over his head, and I hear the soft shirrr as his loin leather comes off. Finally he stands over me, stripped of his raiment, hard, muscular body poised and tense. Only a gold chain glitters briefly in the faint moonlight.

Then he is upon me, heavy and real, his fingers and tongue searching for my secret, sensitive places. Supporting my hips, pulling me upward toward him, his heat between my legs, the unfamiliar fullness, the gorgeous, terrifying wildness of it! My body arches upward, and my head falls back. A deep, guttural moan escapes my throat. "Etiam … sic!"

I hear myself, and at the same moment I hear him whisper, "Anne …"

For an odd moment I dimly feel the schism of two beings at war within me. Part of me wants to stop, to wake up, but he is on top of me, and he is thrusting rhythmically into me, and something is going on inside me that I can't control. Somewhere down in my core a gnawing, aching hollow place needs to be filled. *Etiam! Aye!*

Hunger, possession, surrender, desire—a blur of passions bound together in the white heat of now. I stop thinking. I have come up against my own animal nature, and bald and feral as it is, it drives me on. This body has begun something that it intends to finish.

Clutching, clawing, crying out in the utter savagery of the moment! The muscles and tendons and membranes of my body sing and hum like harp strings, and the reverberations go on and on while I lie there limp and breathless, listening to my own throbbing heartbeat.

When I opened my eyes, it was Mike DeMarco's body that was arching over me in the darkness. His head hung down, and his hair fell over his forehead, shadowing his face. His breath came hard and coarse, and I could still feel his orgasm pulsing inside me. "Marc," I whispered.

His head came up, and he looked at me for a long moment. Then he rolled off and lay there on his back, one upturned hand covering his eyes.

"Mike," I repeated.

"You mean, Marcus?" he said without moving.

For a moment I was confused. I just stared at his profile in the darkness.

He turned to me. "So who was that just now?"

I couldn't answer. I just lay there looking at him.

He threw his legs over the bed and stood up.

"Mike, I know what you must think."

He turned his back and walked a few steps toward the balcony doors. When he spoke his voice was hard. "I think it's great that Daphne got laid. You ought to try it sometime."

"Mike, don't."

"Don't what?" he shot over his shoulder. "Don't try to make love to one woman and then find out it was somebody else completely? Like it doesn't matter? Like one woman is as good as the next?"

"You don't understand."

He turned back to face me. "Explain it to me."

"I wish I could. I don't understand it either, but I do know it was Anne Ryan who came to your bed. I wanted to be near you."

He didn't speak, but I felt his eyes on me.

I held out my hand. "Michael," I said gently, "come back to bed."

He took a few steps and stopped at the edge of the bed. I propped myself up on the pillows and reached for his hand. "Please don't be angry."

"I thought …" He swallowed and tried again. "I thought you wanted me. I thought maybe you were starting to …"

"To love you?"

He nodded.

"Maybe I am. Maybe a part of me does."

"A part's not good enough, Anne."

"I know, but it's all I have right now. Come back to bed. Please."

He sighed heavily and climbed back in beside me. He lay there supine, unmoving, staring at the ceiling. Quietly I reached out and laid my arm across his chest. His hand came up to cover mine. Neither of us spoke. Eventually his eyes closed, and I felt his heartbeat slow.

There was no sleep for me, though. I tried to pray but couldn't concentrate. I gave up and lay there staring up at the ceiling fan that turned slowly above me. When I closed my eyes, the faces of the people I'd just betrayed floated across my mind.

Mother superior … my postulate's vow.

Barry. A year ago he was the only love of my life. Now I was sleeping with a man I barely knew. *Barry, I'm so sorry.*

And Mike. I turned my head to look at his shadowy profile on the pillow next to me. I'd crept into his bed knowing he was falling in love with me, knowing he'd think I felt the same. And now I'd hurt him, too.

I sat up and hung my legs over the side of the bed.

What about Daphne? my voice said.

Daphne?

You entered her life, invaded her most private moments, used her to satisfy your own desires and frustrations.

No!

You slept with her husband.

Stop it!

Selfish bitch, you cheated on them all.

Shut up! Shut up! Shut up!

I took a long breath and listened to the soft whirring of the fan. The voice was gone. All I heard was Mike's breathing next to me. I turned to look at him again. He stirred in his sleep as I watched, and his brows bunched into a troubled frown. I had a momentary impulse to reach over and brush a stray wisp of hair off his forehead. Mike, my only friend. It was probably over now. There was a sadness and sense of loss in that.

But something else was already pulling me away. The hum of Daphne's world was growing stronger as I lay there. She was still alive. There was still time. If I could get back there somehow, maybe I could help her. Maybe I could find a way to save her.

I got up and found my dress, which lay in a heap on the floor. Softly I went over to the balcony and pulled open the doors.

The night was warm and humid, and the trees quivered in a light easterly breeze. I stepped out onto the balcony and eased the glass doors closed behind me. I pulled one of the chairs close to the other one to make a kind of chaise, then I seated myself and put my feet up. Leaning back, I listened to the muffled street sounds, the call of some evening bird, a woman singing softly somewhere in the distance. My head whirled as if I were falling backward.

Interlude XI

I could not summon such passion now, but back then I was overflowing with it. Now all I feel is restlessness.

There is no good in that, Daphne.

Good? There is no "good" here, and no evil. There is only this grey nothing.

There is calm.

I do not want calm! I want to laugh and cry and feel pain and joy and all the things a warm body can feel. I want to hear the laughter of friends and feel the sun on my hair. I want a man's strong arms to hold me in the dark.

Stop torturing yourself. You cannot ...

I want to watch my son grow into a man and have children of his own. I want to grow old and wise. I want to live! Marcus, I wanted so much to live!

I know, my heart. I know.

Now I cannot even cry.

Nor can you live your life through her.

No. But perhaps she can live hers through me, just for a little while.

Chapter 19

"Alexander," I say urgently, "I want that talisman, now!" The child draws back, frowning. "Give it to me, Alexander!"

"But it was a gift from my father!" the boy protests, his eyes welling with tears. "He brought it from the Holy Land!"

"You mean Jerusalem? That is no holy land. It is a land of barbarians, of strange, exotic religions and fanatical priests who preach revolution!" I stretch out my arm. "The talisman, Alexander."

The child steps back. "No! I will tell Father! No!"

"What is going on here?" Marcus says from the door. "What has the boy done, Daphne?"

"I want that talisman he is wearing. He refuses to give it to me." I have not taken my eyes off my suddenly disobedient child.

Marcus's tone is softly ironic. "If you want it, Daphne, I will get one for you as well. I did not know you were interested in such things."

I look up at my husband and feel the hot anger well up like a tide. He is standing there in the doorway, smiling—a complacent, self-satisfied smile. I take two long strides toward my son, reach out, and rip the chain from his neck, drawing a cry of pain and alarm. Then my eyes fix on Marcus's face, which is as startled as the boy's. I address my son without looking at him. "Leave us, Alexander. I wish to speak to your father alone."

The child turns and bolts out the door and down the wooden stairs, his sandals scraping on the boards.

I gather chain and fish into my fist and fling them with all my strength across the room at Marcus. They bounce off his breast plate and skid across the floor. "What do you mean, hanging impious icons around the neck of my son! Are you insane? Do you want to get us all killed?"

"Daphne …" he begins.

"How could you even bring such a thing into this house," I demand, "let alone hang it around your own son's neck?"

"I told him to keep it in his neck pouch. What harm is there?"

"What harm? Those people—those Christians—they refuse to worship the gods! They refuse to sacrifice to the emperor! It is even said that they eat human flesh and drink blood in their rituals!"

"No, Daphne, you do not understand."

"I understand this—the emperor is furious, and so are the gods! The earth has trembled three times in the last month. People are saying it's these Christians who have brought the wrath of the gods down on us. And you would have Alexander walk around wearing their symbol in his bula?"

"Daphne, that is all nonsense. The Christians are no threat to the emperor or anyone else. They are peaceful people. They worship the Jewish god, Jehovah, and follow the teachings of …"

I point toward the corner, where Alexander's talisman lies. "Where did that thing come from?"

"From Jerusalem. From a Jewish woman I visited there, a former prostitute who …"

"A *prostitute*?"

"She was an old woman, Daphne, thin and wrinkled. I was sent there to investigate because people were congregating at her house at night."

"So," I sneer, "she was a whore and a troublemaker."

"She was a holy woman," he says sharply. "She told a story about how she once washed the Savior's feet with her tears and dried them with her hair."

"Disgusting!"

"There were tears in her eyes as she told it. She said this man Jesus had saved her, washed her soul clean. I was moved almost to tears myself."

I advance on him and make a grab for the gold chain I see glimmering on his own neck, half-hidden by his lightweight cloak, but his hand stops me. His fingers close around my wrist and squeeze so hard it hurts. "You are a fool!" I spit at him. "I have waited eight years for a fool!

He releases my wrist and stands looking down at me with dark, angry eyes. "And I have waited for a daughter of Greek philosophers, men who welcomed and embraced new ideas. You disgrace them now with your ignorance and your intolerance. You disgrace me too. If anyone is a fool here, Daphne, it is you."

"Then how did I ever manage all these years without you? At least I am not foolish enough to wear my seditious sympathies around my neck for all the world to see!"

He turns and paces a few steps off, then rounds on me, pointing. "You would still be a pleasure slave in the house of Quintilius if I had not mustered the gold to buy you and free you and marry you! And the wages I sent you all these years have not hurt either, have they? Maybe they were a fool's wages, but they kept you going, did they not?"

"I may have been a slave once," I hiss back at him, "but I am not one now! Not for you or any other man. And you will not come in here after eight years' absence and corrupt our son with your Eastern religions while I am here to stop you!"

His face is almost black with anger. "You are more a slave now than ever! You are a slave to the emperor and his fickle gods!"

I had walked away, but now I whirl on him. "May the gods of Olympus damn you and your Christians!"

For a moment, I actually think he will strike me. But instead he turns, slams through the doorway with his cloak flying, and disappears down the steps. I stand there breathing hard for a few moments, then I cross the room to the balcony window that overlooks the street below. Alexander is there, petting Marcus's big gray warhorse. Marcus comes out of the building and stands on the pavement.

"What is he called?" I hear Alexander ask.

Marcus reaches out and pats the horse's sleek neck. "Plato," he tells the boy. "His name is Plato." The horse nuzzles Alexander's dark brown curls, and Marcus adds, "He seems to like you."

Then Marcus grabs the horse's mane and swings into the saddle. He leans down and says something to Alexander, then he turns the horse's head and rides off down the street.

I turn away and cross to my dressing table. I must visit the baths and purify myself, for I need to go to the temple. I look closely into the polished silver mirror, examining my face. My hair is in disarray, my eyes are hot and bloodshot, and my mouth has a hard set to it that is, admittedly, most unattractive. I do not care. My husband has insulted Aphrodite.

My husband, I think bitterly as I jab a comb into the unruly twist of my hair. Who is this man to tell me how to think, what to believe? And to corrupt our son! To fill his young mind with these treasonous thoughts!

At that moment the door swings open, and I see Alexander in the mirror. He hesitates in the doorway, watching me where I sit, then he starts forward. He stops just behind my chair. "Alexander ..." I begin.

"Forgive me, Mother," he says, and lays his hand gently on my shoulder. "I am sorry I upset you. I will not wear the talisman anymore."

"I just want to protect you, Alexander."

"I know, Mother," he whispers.

"Where has your father gone?" I ask him.

"He went to get provisions. He has to ride to Pompeii this morning. He said I could go with him, if it is all right with you. Is it, Mother?"

"Why must he go to Pompeii?"

"He has been ordered to go. The shaking has damaged some buildings there, and some people might still be trapped in the rubble. He has to go help with the rescue."

I frown. "That might be dangerous, Alexander."

"Father says no, he must just go supervise. He wants me to see how a soldier's work is done."

"Why? Do you want to be a soldier?"

He shrugs. "I don't know. But I would like to go."

Suddenly Marcus is standing in the open doorway. "Alexander," he says sternly, "are you coming?"

Alexander runs to him then turns back to me. The two of them stand there for a moment, the young face eager, the older one still angry. Marcus places his hand possessively on my son's shoulder.

"Do not worry, Mother," Alexander tells me with a grin, "nothing can happen to me if I am with Father."

"Be home for supper" is all I say, and then I turn back to my toilette. I hear the door thud shut and the sound of their footfalls on the wooden stairs.

Chapter 20

The Central Baths, it turns out, are closed today. Something about the water not flowing. Nonsense. Some slave has been derelict, that is all. But I have neither time nor inclination to walk all the way down to the Suburban Baths. I will wash my face and arms in the public fountain near the Forum.

I make my disgruntled way down the walkway from the women's entrance and turn left. I must go back up Cardo IV to the Decumanus Maximus and then down to the Forum, where the Temple of Venus stands. I set my jaw and start off, walking quickly. On my arm is a covered basket that contains three folds of my finest woolen fabric. They are for the goddess, for my offering.

I have only gone a short way before I notice some kind of commotion on the next block. A crowd has gathered, and above the shouts a shrill, squealing sound rises.

Oh, now I see what it is. A mule is loose in the middle of the street. How it got here I cannot imagine—draft animals are not even allowed in this part of town. But there it is, whirling and bucking halfway down the block. It has broken the shafts on its cart and is now frantically trying to kick its way out of the harness. A group of men have encircled the animal while the driver tries to calm it. Even from this distance, I can see its flattened ears, rolling eyes, and bared teeth as it brays in panic.

I have seen this mule before. A big dun with a stiff black brush of a mane. It belongs to Antoninus the wine carter. He has driven it on his delivery rounds for years. It always seemed a placid enough beast before. I wonder what has set it off today.

Another time I might have stopped to watch the outcome of this drama, but I have no patience for it today. At the nearest alley I turn right and follow the narrow lane between the houses until it runs into Cardo V. There I turn east, toward the Forum. Straight ahead looms the mountain, its top lost now in the gathering smoke that continues to pour from its bowels.

The heat is oppressive. I feel it not so much bearing down from above as rising up from the paving stones. The air is thick, close, and a faint sulfuric smell mingles with the tang of the fish market as I near the Decumanus Maximus. Off to the left, the new statue of Hercules rises above the buildings, its colors gleaming in the sun. But I have no time to stop and admire it today.

On the corner stands the fountain. I hurry forward in anticipation of the cool water. But, what is this? The fountain, like the baths, is dry. Not a trickle comes from the spout, and the standing water in the trough is hot and stagnant, as though it has not circulated for hours. There is a strange, acrid smell, too. I cannot allow such water to touch my skin, let alone my lips. Disappointed, I turn right onto the Maximus and quicken forward toward the archway into the Forum.

Aphrodite's temple sits on the eastern side of the plaza near the middle, right across from the temple of Apollo. After the revelry of last night's Vulcanalia, the broad, open space is strangely empty today. A few citizens stand conversing in the shade of the colonnades. A small group of people cluster to watch a sacrificial rite in progress in front of the temple of Pluto. I pass them by and cross directly to the house of the goddess.

By the time I reach the tall, columned building and start up the marble steps, my hair is damp and my skin feels clammy. On the third step I hear what sounds like a great, ominous roll of thunder. I freeze. The sound has come from the mountain. As I turn to the east to look, it comes again, a monstrous, earth-shaking roar, and then an unnatural silence as people in the Forum pause and turn. Oh, something is wrong in Hades. Very wrong. Vulcan is unappeased. All the more reason to seek the goddess's blessing.

The temple's interior is cool and dark once I step through the gilded doors into the large, echoing room. Down at the end, splendid in delicately painted white marble, her gilded hair glowing in the torchlight, is the goddess. The Romans call her Venus, and it is even fashionable to call her Isis in some circles, but I know her by her real name, Aphrodite. She has always been my goddess.

The priestess appears from out of the shadows and comes forward to inspect my gift. She peers into the basket and takes an end of the wool between her fingers, rubbing it, assessing its quality. Satisfied, she steps back and regards me for a moment with sharp gray eyes, then she nods and motions me toward the long double colonnade that leads down the center of the temple.

I move solemnly toward the glowing altar at the foot of the goddess's pedestal. The big, marble ceremonial altar outside under the portico is for blood sacrifice, but this one is for personal offerings, a simple bronze brazier, kept burning with coals. I come to a stop at the goddess's feet and gaze up at her for a few moments. Then I set down my basket, stoop, and take a pinch of incense from one of the porcelain pots on the floor next to it. When I toss the granules into the brazier, a small, green flame rises up, calling the goddess for me.

"Sweet Venus Aphrodite, goddess of my heart, protector of my home and my family, bless us now with your goodness and your love, that we may be cleansed and purified."

I toss in another pinch of incense, and the flame rises higher. Now I reach down and carefully unfold a piece of my soft, newly woven wool. I hold it out to her before laying it on the burning brazier. "Venus Aphrodite, take this gift, the fruit of my labor, for the forgiveness of my husband's error and grant us your blessing and your aid." The wool sizzles in the sacrificial bowl and then begins to burn, slowly at first, then brighter, rising up to the goddess. She has accepted my gift.

The little fire rises higher in the brazier, and I throw on the sweet incense and watch the flames change color. "I pray you, fill my heart with love and understanding. Give me the wisdom and strength to bring my husband back to your favor and your protection. Hear me, gentle goddess, oh great Aphrodite. Take me as your own once more."

I raise my arms to her, gazing into her glittering stone eyes, waiting for her love to wash over me as it always has before. For a moment there is only a humming silence, then I hear something behind me. A woman's voice, murmuring low. I turn.

I am not alone in the temple. Over near the wall, sitting on one of the benches placed there for worshippers, is a woman. A light blue palla covers her hair, but I can see by her strange attire that she is a foreigner. She is moving her hands across her breast and mumbling something in a strange tongue I have never heard before. For some vague reason, she frightens me. The words *You should not be here!* come to my mind as I stare at her.

When I turn back to the altar, what I see shocks me beyond words. Instead of my beautiful goddess, the wooden figure of a crucified man hovers over me. His gaunt, contorted body is covered only by a loose wrap around his loins, and his face in death is hollow and grotesque under a thorny wreath.

I gasp and step back, closing my eyes against the gruesome sight. When I open them again, the man is gone and Aphrodite is back in her rightful place, but I am badly shaken. What is happening? Why am I shown this sacrilege when I have come to her for help?

I bow to the goddess, pick up my basket, and make for the exit, feeling the creep of fine hairs on my neck, the prickle on my back as I step quickly up the center aisle.

When I reach the anteroom, it strikes me as odd that no priestess is there. The foyer is empty, and the golden doors stand ajar. At that instant the marble floor beneath my feet seems to swell and roll like an ocean wave, and I lean on a trembling pillar for balance. Then the motion stops, and I plunge through the doors and out onto the portico. I stand for a moment, blinking and disoriented. The air is filled with ash. I cough and cover my nose and mouth with my sheer white palla.

Then I turn toward the source and am awestruck. As I watch, Vesuvius growls, and the red glow of Hades' fire emanates from its bowels. The top seems to have swollen, like a boil about to burst. And now ash and sparks and fiery rocks have begun spewing from its top. Another deafening explosion shakes the pavement, and then the unthinkable happens.

Priests and worshippers stand stock still in the plaza, staring to the east. A massive column of fire and smoke is now shooting out of the mountain's open maw. As I watch, it begins to rise, up and up and up into the sky, blotting out the sun as it climbs. At its top a vast cloud is spreading outward in a shape like a round-top pine, lopsided now and blowing toward the south, toward Pompeii!

Our familiar, benign Vesuvius has become a huge, ominous black shape against an ashen sky. It should still be midday, but the sky has grown so dark it might be the dead of night. Bits of foamy debris fly all around me, and a hot wind blows my hair loose, whipping it across my face.

I wrench my stinging eyes from the mountain to survey the scene around me. What I see is eerie and bewildering. The Forum plaza is all but invisible now. Under the mountain's roar I hear faint human sounds—a shout, a short scream, a baby's cry, the mad scuffle of feet on stone. Only the flare of a few isolated torches can be seen flying out there like disembodied ghosts. They all fly in the same direction, toward the archway, out of the Forum. I know where they are going. They are running for the harbor.

Marcus and Alexander!

My mind races to catch up with the thought. Surely they heard the roar of the mountain in Pompeii, and that smoke must be blanketing the city! They will be on their way back by now. But where will they go?

The answer comes at once. *Home!*

That is what I've always taught Alexander to do if we should become separated. Go home and wait for me there. That is what he'll do now. I must go home.

I drop my basket, wrap my palla over my face, and start down the marble steps, groping my way in the dimness. When I feel the rougher stone of the plaza under my sandals, I stop again to orient myself. To the right and out through the arch. *Follow the torches.* I start forward, down the length of the plaza toward the Decumanus Maximus. As I run, I am struggling to think. *Where are they now? The ride back from Pompeii will take about an hour. How long has it been since the first explosion? Half an hour? They will still be on the coast road.*

Suddenly a huge white shape looms before me, and I reach out to stop myself. My foot catches, and I go down on a marble step. For an odd, disconnected moment I lie there, confused. Then I look up and realize I am crouching at the base of the portico in front of the temple of Vulcan. Beyond, the temple's polished bronze doors are just visible. *Help me*, I pray silently.

I struggle to my feet and look around. The torches have all gone now, so there is nothing to follow. I must feel my way. The Forum Arch should be just to the right. Feeling with my hands, I follow the edge of the temple's portico to the corner of the building, where I stop again to breathe. The ash chokes me, and I lean against a wall to cough. Holding my veil to my mouth and nose, I pause again to get my bearings.

Yes, there is the arch! At least now I know where I am. Straight ahead past the fountain, a left turn onto Cardo V. Three blocks to home. I can make it.

Chapter 21

I awoke with a jolt, feeling her panic in my chest, in my stomach.

No, Daphne, there's no time!

She was going the wrong way. They wouldn't be in the apartment. By the time she got down to the beach it would be too late. But what could I do? She was already lost, beyond help.

I got up from my makeshift lounge chair and went to the balcony's iron railing. The night was unnaturally still, heavy. Not even the trees stirred. I stood there, scenting the air, my mind racing. Daphne was out there somewhere. I could feel her. But she was going to die. Once more the people I loved were going to die, and I couldn't save them! Here I was, absent again, helpless, waiting for it to happen.

No, something hard inside me said, *not this time.*

I opened the balcony doors, slipped through, and closed them behind me softly, quietly.

This time I would do something.

I tiptoed over to the couch and groped around on the floor where I'd left my sandals. Taking them in my hand, I crossed silently to the door. I was reaching for the knob when something made me stop and turn. Mike was snoring softly over in the corner. He'd thrown off the covers and lay sprawled face-up, looking strangely vulnerable in his nakedness. Part of me wanted to go back to bed, to cover him up and put my arms around him and lie close to him until dawn.

But the other part had to go. She was waiting. I had to help her.

My hand was actually on the doorknob when I heard Mike's voice, deep and urgent. "Vos mos non perdo mihi … ego mos redeo vobis."

It had to be Mike. It had come from across the room. Yet it didn't quite sound like him.

Carrying my sandals I eased over to the bed and peered at his face in the moonlight. His eyes were closed tight, his forehead clenched in an anxious frown. He was sweating, breathing fast. His body jerked slightly as he rolled over. I leaned forward to see his face better. The rapid eye movement was extreme, obvious even in the darkness. He was dreaming. What had he said? I ran a quick translation in my mind and came up with: *You will not lose me. I will come back for you.*

Strange how much he resembled Marcus. Especially in sleep. And the voice … That must be why we'd bonded so quickly.

Stop it. He's not Marcus.

No, of course not. How many times had he made that clear? He was Mike De Marco, his own person. I couldn't drag him into this alternate life I was living. I was in this alone.

"Sleep, Michael," I whispered, so softly it couldn't possibly wake him.

I was turning to go when I noticed something gleaming on the nightstand. I leaned closer to look. His keys! The next thought came too quickly to suppress. *The padlock on the gate to the dig site.* It had to be there!

Slowly, carefully, I slid the chain off the table top and slipped it into the pocket of my dress. Then I crossed the room, opened the door, and stepped out into the musty old hallway. Closing the door quietly, I paused for a moment to slip on my sandals. Then I crept down the stairs to the street.

As soon as I emerged from the building, a strange and eerie sound stopped me on the sidewalk. From somewhere nearby a long, plaintive howl wound its way upward, rising to a peak and then curling downward to a low, throaty growl. Even after the vibrations faded away, the sound lingered on the moist night air. I was still listening to the echo when it came again, hollow and unworldly and yet close, all around me, filling the night. Despite the lingering heat of the day, I suddenly felt cold.

Just a dog, I told myself as I turned down the street. Some lonely neighborhood dog calling out to its kind. Halfway down the block I heard the howl again, farther off. And now an answering sound. Barking, sharp and urgent, coming from somewhere on the next block. I quickened my step as I passed a tiny yard, eyeing the darkness between the houses warily. The dogs of Ercolano were restless tonight.

When I came to the town's main thoroughfare, I stopped momentarily, considering. Straight ahead, a few blocks down, lay the front entrance to the ancient city. But it seemed much more likely that Mike's keys would open the back gate, nearer the dig. He'd taken me that way just yesterday. Of course, it had been daylight then, and now nothing looked familiar. I stood there, trying to visualize. There'd been a side street ... across the way between two shops. Over there. I crossed the street quickly, following blind instinct, and took the first right turn.

The street was narrow and dark, and I could see almost nothing ahead, until I literally ran into the iron bars of the entrance gate. Fumbling in my pocket, I brought out the keychain and searched for a padlock key. There were three small silver ones. On my first try, the key slid into place easily, and the padlock fell open in my hand. I slipped the keychain back into my pocket and gave the bars a tentative push. The gate swung open.

I stood stupefied for a second or two as the realization of what I was doing sank in. I had betrayed Mike's trust, stolen from him. Now I was about to invade a closed archeological site. I was breaking the law! Everything about this was wrong. I could go to jail, or worse, a mental institution.

The phrase *point of no return* came to me. One step farther and my actions would be irrevocable. It wasn't too late. I could still go back, let myself into Mike's apartment, replace the keys, climb back into bed. When I woke up in the morning, it would all be over.

Coward!

Is it cowardice? I asked myself. Or am I, for once, being rational? Or am I just …?

Crazy?

Quite possibly. But I stood at the gates of Herculaneum, and this compulsion was beyond fear, beyond reason or sanity. My own life had been a disaster, but here was a way to make it mean something. Daphne still had a chance. I would be haunted all my days if I didn't at least try to save her.

No, there was no turning back. I took in a deep breath of the dark, alien air, a mixture of Ercolano's life and Herculaneum's dust.

Then I stepped forward.

It was only a few yards to the footbridge that crossed over the old beach and led to the down ramp into the excavation pit. I reached out for the railing, sighed, and stepped out onto the narrow span.

Near the middle of the bridge, I paused for a moment to listen. Dogs were howling all over the city now, and the sound was strangely chilling, like something out of an old horror film. I looked up. There was no full moon, only a high arc of glittering stars surrounding a slender, blue-white crescent. A light wind blew in from the sea, ruffling my hair. Something was niggling at the back of my mind. Something I'd read, about odd animal behavior before natural disasters. Could there be a storm coming?

As I stood there, I heard a deep grating sound and felt the bridge sway under me. Somewhere down there a falling stone hit bottom, and then another, heavier one. I have never felt so acutely aware of my own mortality as I did at that moment—utterly alone, suspended over the ancient harbor on a rickety bridge that still trembled beneath my feet. Every instinct was telling me to go back, to get off the bridge!

Coward!

But what if I can't really help her? What if this is all for nothing?

Weakling, let them die then!
No!
Then you can't stop now. You will not.
I let go of the rail and pushed myself forward.

Negotiating the long ramp to the beach turned out to be a hazard in its own right. Lurching down the slope in the dark, my sandals catching on the stony surface, my hands clutching at the concrete railing, I concentrated on keeping my balance, staying upright. When I reached the bottom, my dress was torn, and the palms of my hands were lacerated. But none of that mattered now. I was alone in the old city at last!

Time had stopped. Past and future were irrelevant. Life as I had known it was over. Only *her* life was real now. And it was her passion that drove me on. I clambered up the first ramp from the beach, ran past the Balbus terrace, and swung onto the second ramp, up the side of the old wall. Full of adrenalin-fueled purpose, I paused only momentarily at the tunnel to catch my breath before hauling myself up the last short ramp and into the town.

Daphne's street was one block over, and I took the shortest route, picking my way between the buildings. Once I turned onto Cardo V, though, a renewed momentum propelled me forward. I flew up the street, scanning the dark for Paulus's bake shop and the outline of her balcony above it. She'd be up there, waiting. I'd get to her somehow.

Just past the third alley I found what I was looking for. Skidding to a stop in front of the bakery, I stood blinking, breathing hard. It was the right place, but something had changed. A long, jagged crack now crept across the graffiti on the wall, and several chunks of loose concrete had fallen on the pavement. I looked up at the balcony. From below it looked sloped, warped.

Then I went to the metal grill and grasped it to look up the stairs. To my amazement, the hasp on the lock came away from the crumbling wall, freeing the rusty gate. It swung wildly, straight at me. The impact of iron against my forehead stunned me for a moment, and I staggered back. When my vision cleared, I saw the gate lying askew, still swinging on its broken hinges.

I looked up the staircase. She was there, I knew it. And now my way was clear. Still I hesitated. I felt my pulse pounding, the fear constricting my lungs. Just for a moment the coward in me longed to be safe, to go back and curl up next to Mike. Yet here I was. And the urge to climb was overpowering.

I grasped the swaying iron gate and took another deep breath. Then I started up the steps, just as another tremor rumbled through. The old wood splintered and gave way beneath my feet, and I reached out to steady myself on the shivering walls. I must have pressed harder than I thought because the wall began to crack beneath my hand. Before I could react, the crack became a jagged fissure, and then a widening hole as the old bricks crumbled. I pushed away just before the wall collapsed in a choking cloud of ancient dust.

Lying face-down on the broken staircase, I shielded my face from the falling debris and waited for the dust to settle. My head ached, and something warm and sticky ran down my temple. I knew what it was, but it didn't matter. I was all right, I could go on. Slowly, painfully, I hauled myself to a kneeling position on the staircase and began to crawl. *Help me,* I murmured as I climbed. *Help me.* Step by step, I dragged my body up, clutching with my jagged fingernails, pushing with my feet, keeping my focus on the second-floor landing just above me. Just a few more steps.

When I finally reached the top of the stairs, I lay for a moment, trying to catch my breath, then I braced myself on what was left of the wall and struggled to my feet. Looking to the right, I could see the door to Daphne's apartment. It was ajar. Inside I could see her dressing table and silver mirror against the wall, her old wooden loom over by the balcony. They weren't charred or destroyed. Neither were the fabrics that lay on the floor nearby. It was all just as it had been.

Some part of my brain knew this was a forbidden threshold I was about to cross, but even as my mind formed the thought, my feet were moving forward. I paused only momentarily in the doorway, then I stepped inside and turned to scan the room. And there she was!

Daphne was on her knees over by the corner, running her hands across the floor, franticly searching for something. Suddenly her fingers clutched at a dark metal object. Carefully she drew it out by its chain, a small, metallic pendant in bronze filigree. I saw her shoulders shake as she pressed the talisman to her lips.

Daphne!

She stopped and froze. Then she turned slowly and looked up, straight at me. In that instant I know she saw me. Her dark, tear-stained eyes fixed on my face. Her body trembled as she rose to her knees. She held up the talisman and whispered something, so soft I couldn't make it out. I opened my mouth to tell her … to warn her … but the words wouldn't come out. *Run!* my mind screamed at her. *Get out of Herculaneum!*

Then I felt myself reeling, losing consciousness, sinking to the floor beside her.

Chapter 22

Chaos reigns on the Decumanus Maximus. In the light of the milling torches, I can see the great statue of Hercules lying in pieces across the intersection. It has toppled from its base and crashed into the fish and produce markets next to Demeter's temple. Down near the Basilica, people are scrambling to crawl over the building's broken columns, falling on top of each other.

Squinting into the gray darkness, I look for the fountain. A few steps, and here it is, under my outstretched hand. Cardo V should be just to the left. But where is it? Nothing looks familiar. And then I see why. There, in the middle of the first block, the upper story of the leather shop has collapsed, along with part of the exterior wall. Rubble is piled several feet high in the street. Screams and cries float out over the rumbling din all around me. Victims are still alive in there, trapped in the smoking debris. Somewhere down the block a donkey brays, and I think of Paulus's two animals tethered to the grinding wheel. But I can help no one. I have to find my family!

There is no getting around these obstacles. Cardo V is totally blocked. My only choice is to follow the fleeing crowd down Cardo IV, cut across at the Decumanus Inferior, and come back up my street from the opposite direction.

I turn left and launch myself into the streaming mass of people heading toward the bay. It is hard to see in the murk, hard to think in this confusion. I let myself be carried along, following the torches, looking for the crossing alleys on my left. And there is the first one! I recognize it by the distinctive carved entrance on the house of Secundus. I stand for a moment, trying to see down the alley, trying to decide if it looks clear.

"Out of the way!" a harsh voice calls out in the gloom. I turn my head to see a torch coming at me. A woman carries a small child over her shoulder as she plows forward. I step aside at the last moment as they push past. There is just time to catch a glimpse of a little girl's blonde hair and an open, wailing mouth before the whirling darkness swallows them up again.

When I look back down the alley, I can see at once that part of the house has fallen. As I watch, the earth shudders again, and a large section of wall crumbles and falls onto the pathway, sending up a cloud of white dust to mingle with the ash from the mountain. The alleys will not be passable. I must move on.

The Decumanus Inferior should be four blocks down. I push on doggedly, moving with the crowd, in a kind of purposeful calm. My mind hunkers down into a tight ball of consciousness, low and determined. I must get home. Nothing else matters.

I am looking for the familiar roofline of the Central Baths, which occupies the corner of Cardo IV and the Inferior. Yes, there it is! Right up ahead! Fighting the flow, I skirt to the raised walkway on the left and feel my way to the corner. Leaning for a moment against a wall, I cough into my palla, then I turn onto the Decumanus.

The Inferior is all but deserted. I run down the wide center avenue in the dark, sensing rather than seeing chunks of debris in my path. The only sound is the mountain's deep, constant roar. The ground shifts again, and I dodge as the flimsy supports for a canopy come crashing down on my right. Up ahead I can see torches and people running across my path. Cardo V is just up there. I see the corner now. The torches are all moving across my line of vision, flowing west toward the tunnel, so I will have to skirt the edge to go back east.

The nearer I get, the more daunting the scene before me. People are fleeing in panic, eyes wide in the torchlight, voices harsh and vicious as they shove each other out of the way. They are a human river surging down Cardo V to the bay, and I must jump in and swim against the current.

I step back against a pillar to catch my breath. The foul air burns my chest as I take in short, jagged gasps. I feel my own heart thudding, the blood pulsing in my ears. I use the edge of my palla to blot the stinging sweat from my eyes. Then I look at the task before me.

Bathed in sickly yellow light, the faces rushing by look distorted, alien, barely human. A family runs through the intersection holding hands, grimly trying to stay together. I watch them disappear into the flow, then I gather myself, step forward, and turn east.

Instantly I am swallowed by the crowd. The debris rains down, and I cannot see where we are going. The narrow street is clogged with frantic evacuees, holding torches aloft as they jostle and bump one another, shouting as they push me with them down the Cardo. For several moments I am swept along helplessly, desperate to stay on my feet, fighting my way against the torrent, pushing and squeezing to get to the side and out of the way.

Then a riderless horse, galloping with the crowd, careens toward me. At the last moment I fling myself sideways and fall to my knees on the cobblestones. My head strikes a concrete wall, and I am stunned for a moment.

A man is speaking urgently to me, pulling on my arm. I have to get away from him. I need to keep moving! But hands are clawing at me. "Let me go!"

"Daphne!" the man shouts. I look up. It is Julius Praxis from the theatre. Three of his slaves stand behind him holding large trunks. They stare at me with wide, terrified eyes. He is hauling me to my feet. "Get up, Daphne! Hurry! We must get down to the harbor!"

"No!" I scream over the uproar all around us. "I cannot!"

He grips my arm and tries to pull me. "Daphne, we must go now!"

I pull away from him. "Leave me!" I cry. "Save yourselves!" I point up the street. "I have to go home! Ego sum subigo praecessi domus!"

The mountain roars, and the ground rolls under us. Praxis stumbles and lets go. He staggers to his feet and looks at me. "May the gods save you," he mouths, and then he turns and runs. The slaves drop their burdens and flee after him.

For a moment instinct tells me to follow. *There is no time ...* a voice inside my head whispers. But Marcus and Alexander may be up there in the apartment right now. They may be waiting for me, worrying about me. I have to go. I steady myself and plunge once again into the fleeing mass of humanity that hurtles to the sea.

Two more blocks. I keep to the side, feeling my way along the buildings under the balconies. As I fight my way eastward, the crowd thins. Only a few desperate people now. A pair of women come stumbling out of a building. I can see one of them is elderly. She screams in terror as a nearby canopy falls. Then the older woman goes down on the cobbles. Her companion pulls on her arm for a moment then turns and runs, leaving her charge in the street. "May the gods save you, Mother," I murmur as I step past her and push on.

I have lost track now, but I think I passed four alleys. Then a familiar shape materializes out of the gloom. Is that my balcony still standing? I stop to peer into the interior of the ground-floor shop. Yes, I can just make out the dim red glow of Paulus's ovens and the faint, lingering smell of baked loaves.

One of Paulus's torches still flickers in its holder inside the door. As I reach for it, I hear a soft whimper. In the dim light, I can just make out a dark lump huddled in the corner. It is Alexander's brown dog, Bellator. In its fear and confusion, the poor creature has returned to the only place of safety it has ever known. The dog raises its head and stares at me questioningly. "Bona fortuna, frater," I whisper. *Good luck, brother.* Then I take the torch and bolt for the stairs.

I am on the first step when another shock rattles the wooden frame on the building. I cry out as a shower of rubble falls down all around me. A chunk of wood falls on my head, and as I stagger sideways, my palla falls off and blows away on the hot wind. I close my eyes and grip the sides of the doorway as the tremor rolls through. Then I start up the wooden staircase. When I reach the top I see the door ajar. "Marcus!" I call as I step inside. "Alexander!"

The room is empty. Holding my torch aloft, I check Alexander's sleeping area, then my own. It is no use. They are not here. I look around frantically. *Where? Where?*

"Where are you?" I scream into the emptiness.

As my eyes scan the room wildly, I try to conjure them. Marcus in the doorway … Alexander standing there, his eyes wide in shock as I yank the chain from his neck … Marcus's hard, angry eyes … What if I never see them again? What if that was the last time?

The chain!

Setting the torch in a holder, I fall to my knees and begin to crawl toward the corner where I threw the talisman, groping before me as I go. My hands follow the floor until I feel something metal near the corner. I draw it out and hold the talisman before my eyes, watching the red light from the mountain flicker against its intricate surface. It looks innocent, fragile, even beautiful with the light playing over its curves.

For this small object I drove away my family. It was so dear to both of them. Perhaps it might have protected Alexander as Marcus said, but I ripped it from my son's neck and threw it away. Here is the bent copper hook. "What did I do?" I moan as I work the soft metal back into shape. "Aphrodite, what did I do?"

And what can I do now? I don't know where to look for them. All I can do is wait here and hope they find me. I cradle the fish in my palm. It feels almost soft in my hand, soft and warm and heavy, like a baby. I raise it to my lips and kiss it gently. "Alexander," I sob. "Alexander …"

Then I hear my own name echoing in the room, soft but distinct. *"Daphne."*

I look up, and there she stands, tall and white and shimmering, her golden hair fiery in the torchlight. I have seen her before. In the temple! In my dreams! Now I know who she is. I crouch there at her feet, arms raised, one hand clutching the talisman and the other reaching out to her. "Aphrodite," I breathe.

Her mouth opens, and words come out. I hear her voice clear and pure, but she speaks in a strange tongue I do not know. I close my eyes and bow my head in homage, and her words come flashing through my mind, quick as thought. *Run! Get out of Herculaneum!* My eyes snap open, and I look up, but she is gone. I do not question. I know what to do.

Clutching Alexander's fish I scramble to my feet. I grab my torch. For a moment I brace myself in the swaying doorway. Then I push away and hurtle down the staircase.

The street is a vision of Hades. Buildings all around me lie in ruins, many in flames. Bits of debris scud across my path and break up in silence, all sound muted under the mountain's constant roar. Looking to the east, I see blue flashes of lightning pulse within the column of fire that now rises, hideous and phallic, into the night sky. The earth lurches beneath my feet, and I drop the torch. I watch it go out as it rolls away. I am utterly alone.

"MARCUS!" I scream into the din. "ALEXANDER!" I stop, trying to think. Where would they go? Where would Marcus take him? And the answer comes to me at once. *The beach, fool!* That is where they are! Orienting myself westward, I turn and run.

As I dodge the fallen rubble, I curse myself for staying too long at the temple. Why did I pause there on the steps when I heard the first blast? Why didn't I run right then? Why did I hesitate at the altar when she was right there behind me, showing me a crucifixion, trying to warn me? How could I be so stupid? *Aphrodite, help me! Help me find my family!*

Passing the corner of the Inferior, I realize that I should have listened to Praxis and gone straight to the harbor. It seemed best to go home and wait for them. Surely they would go there first. Waited too long. Too late now. Hard to breathe ... Too late. All but a few gone. The few who waited too long. *Help me!*

At the end of the cardo the tunnel to the Sacred Area yawns dark and narrow. I hesitate at the entrance, clinging to the hot, slippery stones, chest heaving, eyes burning, seeing nothing but darkness ahead of me. A deep, horrible knowledge squirms inside me. If I enter that tunnel, I will never come out again. This I know with certainty. But they are down there. They must be. There is no other way. *"Aphrodite, help me,"* I whisper. Then I step down.

Instantly I am plunged into absolute blackness and quiet. I cling to the walls and stop. It would be so easy to just sit down, to curl up here and wait for the end. The struggle is too much. I am exhausted. I cannot breathe. I am feeling weak and light-headed. I could sleep here. What a relief to just go to sleep ...

But inside my head a voice chastises. *Coward! You cannot stop now! You will not!*

My goddess is pushing me on. I must do this. I will. I stand up, take a breath, and grope my way down the ramp until I feel the level stones of the first landing under my feet.

Stepping forward, I come out onto the top of the ramp to the second level. There I pause to look over the balustrade at the scene on the beach below. Naval vessels pitching out in the bay, pleasure crafts overloaded and pushing off, fishing boats taking on passengers. Even from the terrace the roar of the surf rivals that of the mountain. Huge breakers, their tops pale and foamy in the dim light of the torches on the beach. People screaming, plunging into the water!

Below me to the right I can see the long plaza of the Sacred Area. Broken pieces of the pergola lie on the ground. The shrines are dark. The priests have abandoned them. Only the high priestess of Minerva remains. There she stands at the balustrade, her purple robes flowing back in the wind, her arms raised to the unyielding skies. Her incantations rise above the tumult around her.

Help me ... I chant as I pass her on my way down the second ramp. *Help me ... help me.*

The stones are wet and treacherous under my feet, and I cling to the sweating walls. A man carrying a child on his back knocks against me on his way down the incline. I pause to catch myself. It is hard to breathe, hard to see. I blink and squint into the glare of torchlight below.

Soldiers on the beach, some mounted and some on foot, shouting orders, loading people onto the few remaining boats. The oarsmen pushing off.

His back is to me, but I know him instantly. He holds a torch while he helps a woman into a small fishing boat. "Quickly!" he shouts. "Subito!"

"MARCUS!" I scream as I scramble down the ramp to the sand. "MARCUS!"

He turns, pulls off his helmet and drops it on the sand. His eyes are wide in the torchlight.

"MARCUS!" I shout again as I run forward.

"Daphne!" He catches me with one arm and holds the torch aloft with the other. "I could not find you! I had almost given you up! Oh, Daphne!" I can hear the despair in his voice.

"Where is Alexander?" I shout above the roar. "ALEXANDER!"

Marcus points out toward the dark and churning sea. "Gone!" he shouts. "I put him on a galley at Pompeii! The captain will look after him! I dared not wait! Had to save the boy!"

I cling to him as another group of panicked evacuees surge forward around us. His neck. It is bare. The gold chain is gone.

"Marc, your talisman? The fish! Where is it?"

"I gave it to Alexander!" he yells.

I hold up the bronze talisman in my hand. My tears are falling on it.

He smiles through his own tears as I reach up to place it on his neck. I am fumbling with the hook when he suddenly straightens and turns his head.

Over the wind and water comes a terrible screaming down at the end of the beach. Women screaming, running toward us.

"Marcus! What can we do? There are no more boats!"

"I have a man going to the shipyards! He will bring us a boat! Maybe big enough!"

"I can take one more here!" the boatman shouts. "Hurry!

"Go, Daphne! Go quickly!"

"No! Not without you!"

"Go! Go, I said!"

"No! We will wait for the next one!"

Marcus wheels to face his manservant, who holds the gray horse. "Go!" he shouts to the boy. "Get into that boat! Swim for it!"

The boy bolts, and Marcus grabs the reins. From the town comes a great, thundering roar and wild screaming. "You!" Marcus shouts. "Soldier! Get the rest of these people into the boat chambers over there! Here, take my horse. Save him if you can! Hurry!"

I see the troops marching into the archways, driving the few straggling civilians ahead of them. The pale horse disappearing into the darkness …

"Look!" Marcus points. "Here comes our boat! Hurry, man! Hurry!" He turns to me. "You stay here, Daphne! Stay here, do you understand? Wait for the boat!" He stoops for his helmet. "I am going to see if I can get to those women. They are locked out of the chambers down there!"

"Marcus, NO!"

"I cannot just leave them! Wait! I will hurry!"

"I love you!"

He kisses me quick and hard, and his arm tightens around me for a moment. Then his hand is gentle on my face. "Be brave, girl," he says below the turmoil.

He straps on his helmet and turns to go. I grasp his arm. "Marcus, I cannot lose you!"

He turns back to me and shouts into the wind. "You will not lose me! Ego mos redeo vobis! *I will come back for you!*" And then he is gone into the night. The women screaming, running toward him … the boatman pulling on my arm … the roar deafening … the heat!

"MARCUS!" I scream after him. "COME, MARCUS … HURRY!" He turns his head as he runs and casts me one last look, then he's gone. Hot wind! The priestess falling, flailing as she drops! Cannot breathe. "MAR-CE!"

A cinder strikes my forehead and sears its way into my skin. Then a blast of wind blows me off my feet. I fly backward onto the sand, and the impact stuns me. Now I feel my skin shriveling, my eyes scorching. I am blind! Writhing! MAR … Muh … MAAHHHHHhhhh!"

Interlude XII

It is coming clear to me now. She was not a daemon, not a goddess. She was just a woman like me, a wife and mother, lost in time. And I found her.

   Or did she find you?

Both, I suppose. We were both seeking to escape our fate. She was reaching backward in time, and I was reaching forward, and we found each other here, in this place where there is no time.

   But why you, Daphne? Why would she come to you? And why now?

Because of what we'd both lost. A husband, a son, all we loved in the world. We were both in the extremes of desperation when we came together. She was lost in her grief—frozen there, unable to go on. And I was also trapped. The thread of my life was cut off at the peak of anguish. Do you see? We needed each other, and the Fates brought us together when she started to dream.

   You were dreaming of her, too.

Yes. I must have felt her coming from a long way off.

It was not so easy for me.

What?

He never came to me, not even halfway.

Marcus, what are you saying?

I had to break through all his defenses. But I am a soldier. I understand defenses.

You went to Michael? You never told me this!

I was not sure. But when he spoke in his sleep, when he told her he would come back for her and she heard him, that is when I knew.

Oh, Marc, I love you.

Ego vos amor, cara mea.

Chapter 23

I awoke in a hospital room. A young nurse in crisp blue scrubs was sponging my forehead. "Welcome back," she said in American English.

"Where am I?" I asked her.

"US Naval Hospital in Naples. You were brought in last night. I guess you got caught in that earthquake in Ercolano. Had some kind of seizure? Do you remember?"

I shook my head. I remembered pieces of it. The gate and the bridge ... the ramps ... the staircase ... Daphne ... But I couldn't imagine how to explain it to this nurse. Instead I asked, "Am I okay?"

"You seem to be, but the doctors are still running tests." She dipped her sponge in a pan of cool water and squeezed it. "You were suffering from severe hyperthermia when you came in, and you were having trouble breathing."

"I've got a screaming headache," I told her.

"Here," she held out two white pills and a cup of water. "This'll help."

I took them and lay back on the pillow.

She was dabbing at my forehead again. "Do you have a history of seizures?"

"No."

"Hyperventilation?"

"No."

"Nothing like this had ever happened to you before?"

I shook my head and winced.

"Hmmm," she said, "weird." She studied me for a moment before setting the sponge and basin on her rolling cart.

I didn't answer.

"So you feel like some company?" she asked me with a little smile.

I frowned. "Company?"

"The guy who brought you in. He's been waiting here all night." Then, as if to tempt me, she added with a smile, "Good lookin' man."

When I nodded, she winked and turned for the door. "I'll get him."

Mike came in with a red rose wrapped in tissue. He handed it to me then pulled up a chair and sat looking at me. I smiled weakly and reached out my hand to take his.

For what must have been a minute or so, nobody spoke. He just sat there, his face still, his eyes uncomfortably direct. I found it hard to meet them.

Finally the silence was too much. "Mike," I began, "about your keys …"

He nodded. "I found them in your pocket."

"I'm sorry."

Another silence ensued.

Eventually I looked up to find him still studying me. His eyes looked tired, and there were little worry lines between his brows.

"How do you feel?" he asked.

"Tired," I said, "and I've got a headache. But otherwise, I guess I'm okay."

"I thought you were dying."

"Part of me was, I guess."

"Daphne?"

I nodded.

His face remained impassive.

"I was there, Mike. I went through it all with her. Right to the end."

"Why did you do that?" he asked me. "Why did you go down there alone?"

"I wanted to save her."

He gave me a level gaze. "And did you? Save her?"

My answer came so fast I didn't have time to reason it out. "In a way."

He frowned. "What do you mean? She died, Anne."

"Yes, of course, nothing could save her from that, but ..."

"But what?"

"She saw me," I blurted. "Just for an instant."

"Anne ..."

"No, she saw me, Mike. I know she did."

He stared at me.

I continued as the thought slowly crystallized in my head. "If I hadn't been there, she might have waited too long. She'd never have made it to the beach. She wouldn't have seen Marcus. She would have died alone, in her apartment, not knowing about her son." I looked up at him, a smile curling my lips. "I helped her. I really did."

He reached into his pants pocket and pulled out a small object wrapped in tissue paper. "You were holding onto this. It was all we could do to pry it out of your fist."

He handed me the little bundle, and I slowly unwrapped it, knowing what it was. The talisman lay heavy in my hand. It still felt hot. My fingers slowly traced its dark, intricate contours. It wasn't a phantom, it was hard and smooth and solid. The tears came in short, jerking spasms as I pressed it between trembling hands and brought it to my lips. I looked up at Mike through blurred eyes. "It was real," I choked out. "She was real! I'm not crazy!"

His gaze was more intense than I'd ever seen it. "Where did you get that?"

"She gave it to me," I said, smiling through the tears.

"What does that mean? She gave it to you?"

"I mean, I found it. At her apartment."

"Where exactly?"

"The insula on Cardo V, across from the Palaestra."

He blinked at me for a moment. "You were up there?"

I nodded. "The gate was open."

"You know, that whole building collapsed last night."

I stared at him, speechless.

"That was a 5.9 earthquake you ran out in."

I stroked the talisman with my finger. "This might have been lost forever."

"You might have been lost forever."

"I know."

"Was it worth it?"

I nodded. "Yes."

He held out his palm. "Let's see it again?"

I handed it over and watched him turn it slowly with his fingers. "It doesn't look Roman," he finally said. "More Middle Eastern. Eastern Mediterranean maybe."

"It came from Jerusalem." I took a ragged, halting breath. "It has an amazing history. A biblical history!"

"Biblical?"

"Oh, Mike, there's so much I have to tell you!"

"I'm listening."

I hesitated, puzzling over a disjointed series of images that all came flooding in at once. *Marcus standing there, trying to explain … the talisman gleaming in the torchlight ….and then out of nowhere, an old woman, her face half-lit in dim light, holding out her hand, offering something …*

I shook my head. "Not now." I looked up apologetically. "It's all fuzzy and vague. I guess I'm just tired."

He gave my arm a gentle squeeze. "Tell me tomorrow, then. I should go anyway. Visiting hours are almost over."

He started to get up, but I put out a hand to stop him. "Don't go just yet."

"I don't want to wear you out."

"Just a little longer, until I fall asleep."

He sat back down. "Okay."

I examined his face. It seemed more hollowed, more shadowy than before. There was a tightness around his eyes. "You look pretty tired yourself," I told him.

"I was up all night." He rubbed the bridge of his nose and shook his head. "It's been a rough twelve hours."

"I know."

When he looked up, something like accusation sparked in his eyes. "I woke up and you were gone. When I found you down on the beach, I thought you were dead. I was scared as hell. I couldn't get any help."

"You found me at the excavation site?"

"Yeah, in the pit."

"How did you get me out of there?"

"I carried you."

Suddenly it came to me just what I had put him through. The dark, treacherous climb up that long ramp and over the swaying footbridge carrying an unconscious woman, then the struggle down dark, empty streets with rubble falling all around. He'd been utterly alone in the middle of an earthquake. He must have been exhausted, near collapse himself. But he'd brought me out, somehow gotten me to a hospital. I owed him my life.

"Mike," I said, "I'm so sorry. How can I ever thank you enough?"

His eyes held mine steadily. "Love me."

The emotion rushed up from my chest into my throat. "Michael ..." I breathed, and I opened my arms to him.

He fell into them. His body pressed into mine on the pillow. When he spoke, his voice was thick with feeling. "I don't want to lose you."

I held him and stroked his hair and kissed his face. "Oh, I don't want to lose you either."

He sat up suddenly. "Then don't go. Stay here with me for another month, and then we'll go back to Michigan together." When I didn't respond, he added, "Anne, we could have a life."

The words "I do love you" rose almost to my lips and then subsided.

Run, my voice whispered, *it's a trap.*

Yet there he was, real and alive, holding me with those dark, liquid eyes.

But what if you love him and he …?

Mike sat waiting while I gripped his hands and fought my inner war. He was right here, right now. So close. I was so close …

What if he …?

He sat there still as water. I could see my reflection in his eyes.

Dies! The word hissed through my brain and slithered down my nerve endings.

The old familiar shadow fell across my heart. My stomach was tightening, and my breaths came short and irregular. I felt myself retreating, fending him off.

I raised his hands to my lips and kissed them. "Michael, I have to go. Please understand. This has all happened too fast. It's all jumbled up in my mind. I need time to sort it out, make some sense of it."

I watched him wrestle with an argument for a few seconds, then his eyes dropped. He sighed. When he looked up again, it was with resignation. "So where will you go? Back to Michigan?"

"For a while. I thought maybe I'd rent a little beachside condo in Saugatuck or South Haven or someplace like that. Just for a few weeks, until I get my bearings."

He nodded. I couldn't quite read his expression. His face was beginning to blur. My eyelids were so heavy.

"Hey, you okay?" I heard him ask.

I nodded. "It's … the sedative."

"Should I call the nurse?"

A great fatigue was settling over me, a desire to sleep. Just sleep. To be at peace.

"Anne?" His voice seemed far away.

"I'm just so … so…" I felt my eyelids flutter closed, and I sighed.

His hand caressed my brow. "Sleep then," he said softly.

I am spiraling through darkness. There is no fear, only a vague sense of time stretching and bending. Marcus is here. I can't see him, but there's a hint of his rich, musky scent...

"Don't go," I murmur.

"It's okay," Mike's voice said. "I'm right here."

⊕ ⊕ ⊕

Mike rode with me in the cab to the Naples airport. The afternoon heat had given way to a sudden downpour, and we sat in the backseat, dripping and uncomfortable. Neither of us spoke, but quietly he laid his hand, palm up, on the seat next to me. I took it and continued gazing out the rain-streaked window at the passing streets. What was there to say? Leaving was harder than I'd expected.

At the baggage check-in line, we stopped and stood in strained silence, holding hands, avoiding each other's eyes until the announcement came over the loudspeakers, first in Italian and then in English: "Ladies and gentlemen, Al Italia flight 103 to New York is now ready for boarding."

I looked up at him.

"That's your flight," he said quietly.

I nodded.

His eyes searched mine for a moment, then he touched my hair, holding a lock between his fingers. "Call me when you get back to the States?"

I nodded again. My throat was tight, and I was finding it hard to talk. Instead I reached up, took the hood of his jacket in my grasp, and pulled his mouth forward so I could reach it with my lips. For a moment his rain-damp body melted against mine, and we stood, locked together, oblivious to the stream of moving humanity eddying around us. But finally a woman with a baby knocked into us, excused herself, and broke the current. I touched him once more with my lips, and as I did, I slid a small, tissue-wrapped package into his jacket pocket. Then I bent to gather up the small carry-on bag he'd lent me. He was still standing there, stoic and desolate, when I turned to give him one last wave before disappearing down the concourse.

Taxiing toward the runway, I leaned forward to look out the window. Through the slanting rain I could just make out a hooded figure standing alone on the observation deck. *Forgive me, Michael,* I whispered silently. *I'm not what you need.*

My inner voice answered with customary brutality. *Coward!*

I closed my eyes as the plane took off, felt the jolt as the wheels left the tarmac and the sudden upward lurch, heard the grinding sound and felt the soft shudder of the landing gear retracting. As we began a slow bank over the airport, I gazed down at the city of Naples and the verdant Italian countryside beyond as it gave way to the curving coastline and then the endless, slate-colored water topped with churning whitecaps. Finally, all of that disappeared, too, and we came up through the clouds to a billowy white world of peaks and valleys and empty blue.

Don't say anything, I told my voice. *Leave me alone.*

But, of course, she couldn't do that

Here we go again … another self-imposed exile.

Interlude XIII

We have done our best, Daphne. She must take herself the rest of the way—if she can.

I worry for her still, but I am weary, husband.

It is time for us to leave this place.

But, Alexander …

You were right, mea cara. You were always right. He has gone on.

Marcus, when did you come to this?

I suppose I have always known. He would have come long ago.

If that is so, then he must have …

Aye, he must have survived.

He was never trapped here.

No.

Oh, be it so!

Perhaps he became a soldier.

Or an actor.

*An **actor**?*

A playwright, then.

Or a naval officer.

Gods forbid, a weaver.

No, he was strong and vigorous. He would be a man of action.

He was also quick of mind. Perhaps a philosopher, a teacher.

Whatever he became, cara, he took part of us with him into the future.

Yes.

Then it is well.

We can go now.

Not quite yet. There's one more thing I must do.

Chapter 24

The resorts along Lake Michigan are quiet in September. Saugatuck's summer tourists have gone, and the leaves are turning yellow and orange. The water is too cold for swimming now, but the beaches are still soft and golden in the afternoons.

I walk a lot. Often I stroll the tree-shaded streets with their quaint storefronts, peering idly into the shop windows—candles, glassware, souvenirs. I rarely buy anything; I just have this compulsion to walk, to keep moving. It's therapeutic in a vague sort of way.

Of course, there are reminiscences. Barry and I used to come here. We walked these same streets that summer I was pregnant with Sean. The memories are bittersweet, but I'm learning not to shut them out. They're part of me.

Sometimes I go down to the marina and watch the sailboats bobbing on the water, their furled masts rocking against the sky. My parents had a slip here for our boat, the *Annie Liz*. I like to walk out to the end of the pier and stand there, the wind snapping my jacket, the deep blue breakers rolling in and smashing against the bulkheads with a cold, rhythmic chop. Daddy was so happy out on the water. I can still see his grin as he trims the sails. Mom laughs and holds on to Bobby as we heel and come about. These are my loved ones. I don't want to forget them.

But it's not just my ghosts I'm learning to accept. I've needed this time alone with myself, to get to know Anne Ryan again. I'm still me—still the orphan, the young mother, the widow, the nun—but there's someone else here, too. Memories of Daphne no longer haunt me in dreams or visions. She lives inside me now like some prodigal Other home at last.

Daphne unveiled the deepest levels of my nature and mirrored them back to me. Her passions and her ecstasies are part of me now. I must admit, I'm not altogether comfortable with this new flood of feeling. It's much harder to control my emotional impulses than it used to be. I suppose that's a good thing. Probably. When I get used to it.

I am clearer about some things, though. It's finally dawned on me that before I can fully live in the present, I must come to terms with the past—mine as well as Daphne's. Back in Herculaneum I'd been convinced that she needed me, that I could somehow reach back two thousand years and save her from her fate. But that's where I was deluded. For all my determination, I could no more undo her tragedy than I could my own. The past is the past. You can relive it over and over if you choose, but you can't change it.

Looking back at it now, I realize that she was driving the course of events, not me. I didn't lead Daphne to the beach; she led me. It was for my sake that the two of us made that journey together down the dark, chaotic streets, into the yawning blackness of the tunnel, and down the ramp to the beach. She took me right into the mouth of death with her. I saw its eyes, felt its breath. It nearly swallowed me. But unlike Daphne, I survived.

She had wanted so much to live. Everything about her was vivid, immediate, intense. She was fully there every moment. I felt her fighting for life even as the avalanche overtook her. And yet, I was the one who came through it. I, who have spent so much of my own life dwelling on death, almost romanticizing it. A sad irony. But no amount of regret, no amount of grief, no amount of atonement can change the past.

You can change the future, though. Unlike Daphne, I still have time, and to waste the precious hours and minutes I've been given would be a sin. I can't go back, and I can't stand still; I can only go forward. But where? Where should I go?

I find myself more than usually unsettled today. When I got back from my evening walk on the beach yesterday, I found a message on my cell phone.

"Hi, Anne, this is Mike. Sorry I missed you. Just wanted to let you know I'm back in Ann Arbor now. I thought about calling sooner, but you said you needed space, so … Anyway, I was thinking maybe I could drive over this weekend, and we could have lunch or something. If you want to, I mean. If you don't, that's okay, but I really would like to talk to you. I'll try you again tomorrow night. Okay, I guess I'll talk to you later, then. Bye."

I've played the message over and over. Several times I've even picked up my phone, scrolled to the cell number he gave me at the airport, and punched it in. But every time my thumb goes to hit "talk," something stops me. It's like I'm tiptoeing the edge of some invisible borderline and one step in any direction could tip my balance. Somehow talking to Mike feels like that kind of step. I can't seem to bring myself to take it.

Still, his voice tugs at me, I can't deny that. When I heard it yesterday, some dormant part of me surged to life again. Listening to his message, I closed my eyes and was back in Ercolano. I felt that flutter in my stomach again, the enlivening of every nerve. The woman in me wants to see him, to be with him. But is it really Mike I want? I have to be sure. Especially now.

Fortuna's wheel has turned once again. I knew it even before I took the early pregnancy test last week. I just felt different. Somehow the four of us managed to conceive a child that night in Ercolano.

Alexander.

Or Alexandra.

A new life, an old soul. If I talk to Mike, if I see him again, I'll have to tell him. He has a right to know. But what then? What if he thinks I'm trying to trap him and withdraws? How awful to see the warmth in his eyes fade, to see them grow distant and evasive. But what if he wants to get married and be a family, the three of us? Can I commit to that? Can I start all over again?

I don't know. I really don't. It scares me.

I want this child, there's no doubt. But, after all that's happened, am I fit to be a mother? Would I raise a strong, healthy, confident child, or would my anxieties make me cloyingly attentive, overprotective, smothering? Would my child grow up to be an emotional weakling?

And what about marriage?

Mike has so much to offer. Yes, there's physical attraction, but that's not all. We only had a few days together, but our minds were so connected that we finished each other's thoughts. He's brilliant, and he's honest, and he loves me. Despite his youth, he's one of the best men I've ever known, and he deserves far more than I've been able to give. At the very least he deserves a woman who can call him by his own name. Why he still wants anything to do with me is a mystery.

But the question is what do I really have to offer him? I told myself the fear had faded away. I had named it, faced it, debunked it. But last night when I held the phone in my hand with my fingers poised over the keys, ready to call him back, there it was, that old familiar dread at the prospect of emotional vulnerability. Would this weakness make me forever guarded and reticent, always holding back, avoiding real intimacy? Or maybe I'd go the other way and become clingy and insecure. Maybe I'd be one of those women who makes her husband feel guilty every time he steps out the door. To what extent can conscious intention override unconscious impulse?

Love me, he said. *We could have a life.*

Yes, but would it be a happy life? Am I even capable of happiness, or would I just end up draining all the joy out of him?

I can't be sure.

A few things have crystallized, though, in the course of my reflections. I've come to recognize something dark in myself. The truth is, for a long time, maybe even before Barry and Sean died, some part of me has always distrusted happiness. Love is a joy that carries the highest of price tags—a bauble that fate holds out with a smile, only to snatch it away, laughing, just when you've come to need it, depend on it.

Mike doesn't understand that. He associates love with life, not death. He wants it, believes in it, trusts it. He's never had to face the loss of it. Braced by that innocence, he can blithely risk everything. But fate will have her price. And it's high. Oh, Michael, it's so high!

Something hard and tight rises in my chest, and suddenly I'm short of breath.

Stop, my inner voice says. *Stop thinking.* She is kinder to me now than before, less punishing. *Rest,* she whispers. *Just be.*

Over there, right at the shoreline, half-buried in sand, lies an old piece of driftwood where I like to sit and watch the waves. I go there now and settle myself on a long, flat limb that hangs over the water. Slipping off my sneakers, I stretch my toes out to the rising foam as the evening tide comes in.

As it often does, my mind flashes on Daphne's talisman, the fish. The one tangible thing I had from her. Sometimes I second-guess giving it away. Sometimes I wish it were right here on its chain around my neck, where I could see it, touch it, reassure myself. It was meant for me, I know. But back at the Naval Hospital, when I put it on and tried to wear it, the weight of it and the residual heat it gave off were too much. I tried putting it in a small box by my bedside, but even then, when I took it out to hold it and look at it, all I could feel was her horror and her pain. I didn't want to remember Daphne that way.

Besides, it was the least I could do for Mike, for all he'd been through with me. It's a significant archeological find. It will add great weight to his dissertation. It belongs in a museum, anyway, where others can see it and be inspired. I know she'd understand.

Now I wear the small gold cross my mother gave me for my first Communion. It lies so softly against my skin. I no longer need stone and candles and stained glass. I don't need to hear the ancient Catholic rituals and the soaring music. But I miss those things. When I leave this haven, I will find a beautiful old church where I can go and pray and meditate.

But sitting here on the shores of Lake Michigan, gazing out over the blue expanse, I feel God. He is here. For the first time in my life,

I feel a real and immediate presence when I sit quietly in the midst of his Creation. I'm no longer angry. I no longer blame him for my misfortunes. God is not up there in that cloud waiting to rush to my rescue when I summon him. It is for me to reach up, and out, and down into myself, to approach him as nearly as I can in this lifetime. I've reread the scriptures, I've prayed, and I've contemplated. The one overarching idea that keeps coming back to me is that love is the key. Despite everything, love.

This is the monologue that plays in my head as I sit here on this piece of driftwood. At the same time, I find myself reveling in the world of physical sensation—the wind on my face, the rhythmic crash of waves, the smell of dune grass and fish, the cool water lapping at my bare feet.

My far-flung gaze follows a pair of gulls in their wide, arcing path over the beach. They call to each other then bank in perfect unison and head out over the open water to some destination unknown.

Out there on the wide, curving horizon thousands of tiny mirrors wink on the sun-dazzled water. My mind snaps picture after picture, trying to capture the moment, knowing tomorrow it will exist only in memory. But the wind has shifted. It blows steadily out of the west now, raising bumps on my bare arms. The sun is low in the sky. Time to move on.

I slide down from my perch, untie my jacket from around my waist, and slip it on. My feet are wet, so I just pour the sand out of my shoes and carry them as I set off down the beach. Up ahead a line of grassy dunes forms a low promontory jutting out to follow the slow curve of the shoreline. The view from up there is spectacular. That's where I'm headed.

I climb the dune and stand at the top. The wind catches the sheer blue veil that covers my hair, and I feel it come loose. I reach up to save it as it blows in the breeze. Then I feel the warmth of the sun on my hair.

Anne, my voice asks. *why do you need a veil?*

The answer comes too quickly. To cover myself.

What are you covering?

I don't know.

Yes, you do.

It's way down there. I can't get to it.

Do you want to?

Yes.

Let it go, Anne.

The breeze off the lake picks up a liberated lock of hair and sweeps it across my cheek. I raise my arm and hold the fragile piece of fabric to the wind. It tugs, but for a few seconds I hold on, hesitant to let go. Then I open my hand and watch the veil sail upward, fluttering and whirling on the air currents, until it disappears into the blue of the sky. The bright hair blows around me like a fire. I am free.

Walking back, the voices play in my head.

"Have courage. Live!" I see his face as he said it, urgent and full of passion, dark eyes glowing in the candlelight. Michael …

"Love me."

The old program kicks in automatically. *But love is a trap … a trap … a trap …*

I should know. I've survived it three times now.

The next thought stops me on the sand. *I'm a survivor!*

I stand there surveying the long sweep of shoreline stretching before me. I am utterly alone on the beach. And I'm okay.

Now, sitting here on my little deck overlooking the water, I watch blue dusk slowly eclipsing the last strokes of sunset. The red sun ignites the horizon in a blaze of liquid fire. I feel drowsy. The Indian summer day, the sun and the sand and the wind, have made me pleasantly tired. I wrap myself in a quilted throw and lie back on my lounge chair. The soft lap of the waves lulls me. I feel myself drifting. With a sigh, I let go …

⊕   ⊕   ⊕

I am walking on the beach at night. Searching for someone. The wind howls, and the surf pounds, and I am afraid. I do not know this place.

Then, down the beach, a figure appears out of the gloom holding a torch aloft. Under his arm he carries a centurion's helmet. Its curved bronze surface glints in the firelight as he strides toward me with a rhythmic, military gait. I start running down the strand, faster... faster... Just as I reach him, he casts off the helmet and catches me with one arm.

"Marcus!" *I cry as I cling to him.* "Oh, Marcus!"

The torch flies away. He holds me in his strong embrace for a moment then straightens and locks his eyes onto mine. "I came back for you."

"Marcus, I never stopped loving you. Not for a moment!"

"I never doubted it."

"Forgive me," *I whisper against his neck,* "for what I said ... what I did."

He raises my chin. His eyes are dark and gentle. "Dearest heart, I forgave you that so long ago. But when will you forgive me?"

"For what?"

"For leaving you."

For an instant his meaning swirls. They all flash before me. Mom, Dad, Tommy piling into the SUV, waving as they drive off ... Barry and Sean standing in the garage grinning as I back out the drive ... Marcus strapping on his helmet for the last time, casting me one last look before turning to race off down the beach .... I can't breathe!

He gathers me back into his arms and strokes my hair. "Do not be afraid. You are not alone."

The pounding of the surf calms as I press myself against him. "No, not as long as you're here with me."

"I've been with you all along, Annie," *Barry says.*

"Yes," *I sigh.* "Yes."

"But now you have to open your heart."

I look up into his face, and his intent pierces me like a sword. "No! Don't ask me."

A deeper voice says, "Be brave, girl."

"I can't ..." *My voice is muffled against his chest.* "I can't ..."

"Yes, you can," *Marcus says.* "Your heart is stronger than you know."

"But if it breaks again ..."

"Then you will survive again."

His words hang for a moment on the ether, not flying away and not sinking in, simply waiting.

"Anne, it'll be okay," says a new voice. "Trust me."

This voice wraps itself around me like a soft quilt. The sea grows quiet around us. His body is warm against mine, light but strong. His breath is on my hair.

"I do," I sigh. "I do trust you."

Marcus takes my face in his hands and smiles as he kisses me. "You are the most beautiful woman."

"I won't always be beautiful, you know."

His eyes glow at me, soft and dark and full of love. "You will always be beautiful to me."

Finally my fear surrenders. I reach up to kiss him. His lips are warm and real, and, for an instant, they taste faintly of spearmint.

We stand there clinging to each other while the surf rolls to shore, then Marcus takes me by the shoulders. "Daphne," he says gently, "I have come to say goodbye."

The words thud into my chest. "But where are you going?"

"You know." His eyes are deep and grave.

A sudden horror overtakes me. "Back ... there?"

He is receding. "Back where I belong." His form begins to blur.

"Marcus, no!" The waves come crashing in, their fractal rhythm rising, insistent. "Stay with me!"

"I cannot." His voice echoes, fainter. "You know that."

"Then take me with you!"

He shakes his head slowly, solemnly.

I feel the panic rising. "I can't lose you! Not again!"

"You did not lose me," he calls. "I said I would come back, and I did!"

"Mar-ce!"

His lips move, but I can't hear his words anymore. All I hear is the roar of the waves and the strangled cry that struggles to escape my throat. I open my mouth to force out the scream, but I cannot seem to make the sound.

His whisper comes back to me on the wind. "Live now. Live!"Even as I strain to hold on, his face is changing, becoming younger, finer featured.

"Michael ...?"

"He does not know,"Marcus says as he fades into the darkness,"but his soul does."

⊕　⊕　⊕

A jangling sound comes from afar and brings me back.

Marcus is gone. The night breeze, the surf, the distant call of a gull—these are real, physical. This is me. This is now.

The ringing comes again. I know what it is. It's Life calling.

I rise to answer.